Jonathan Hutchinson

The pedigree of disease

Being six lectures on temperament, idiosyncrasy and diathesis

Jonathan Hutchinson

The pedigree of disease
Being six lectures on temperament, idiosyncrasy and diathesis

ISBN/EAN: 9783742806048

Manufactured in Europe, USA, Canada, Australia, Japa

Cover: Foto ©Andreas Hilbeck / pixelio.de

Manufactured and distributed by brebook publishing software
(www.brebook.com)

Jonathan Hutchinson

The pedigree of disease

THE

PEDIGREE OF DISEASE

BEING

SIX LECTURES

ON

TEMPERAMENT, IDIOSYNCRASY AND DIATHESIS

DELIVERED IN THE THEATRE OF THE ROYAL COLLEGE
OF SURGEONS IN THE SESSION OF 1881

BY

JONATHAN HUTCHINSON, F.R.S.

Late Professor of Surgery and Pathology in the College; Emeritus Professor of Surgery in the
London Hospital; President of the Ophthalmological Society, etc., etc.

NEW YORK
WILLIAM WOOD AND COMPANY
56 & 58 Lafayette Place
1885

THE PUBLISHERS
BOOK COMPOSITION AND ELECTROTYPING CO.
157 AND 159 WILLIAM STREET
NEW YORK

PREFATORY NOTE.

WITH a few emendations I have reprinted these Lectures just as they were delivered in June, 1881, and as they appeared at the time in one of the medical journals. I am well aware of their many imperfections, but am hopeful that they may be found to point to work in the right direction. It was, indeed, the commendation which this method of dealing with some of the problems of disease received from Sir James Paget, in his Bradshaw Lecture of last year, which induced me to determine on their present publication.

THE PEDIGREE OF DISEASE.

LECTURE I.

MR. PRESIDENT AND GENTLEMEN,—I fear I do not much mistake in the belief that the subjects which I have ventured to take for my present course of lectures are by no means high in professional favor. Our forefathers, who knew far less about the details of pathology than we do, attached far more importance to such matters as temperament and diathesis. They were accustomed to prescribe for a man's temperament; we think only of his disease, and turn aside with weariness from classifications of diathesis in which the physicians of an older day delighted. Although to a large extent this change of sentiment has been the result of advance in knowledge, yet I think it might easily be shown that it has gone too far, and that we now neglect unwisely the study of those differences between man and man of which, for the most part, physiology takes no cognizance, but which may yet prove of much importance in modifying the processes of disease. It is to this study that I now invite your attention. I have been attracted to it in part by its own intrinsic interest, and in part by the circumstance that it has seemed to be, in some sense, supplementary to the lectures which on former occasions I have had the honor to deliver from this chair. In my first course (three years ago) I investigated the present state of knowledge as to the influence of the nervous system in the production of disease. In the second we examined those remarkable and widely-spread forms of diathesis known respectively as Gout, Rheumatism, and Leprosy. When on these subjects I tried to show that rheumatism is a modification of the catarrhal diathesis, mainly nervous in its origin, in which the stress of the reflex disturbance falls upon the tissues of the

1

joints. I traced a close parallel between gout and leprosy, alleging that both are food-diatheses, being distinctly and definitely caused by certain peculiar articles of diet. Respecting both we had to remark upon the facts, that having been thus acquired by food, they became capable of transmission from parent to child, and that gout, at any rate, was prone to receive important modifications in such inheritance. In my third course, delivered last summer, I was led by a not unnatural sequence to take as my topic the laws of pathological inheritance in general, and to deal with them in relation to such maladies as syphilis, gout, leprosy, catarrh, and certain specialized defects, such as deaf-mutism, color-blindness, and hæmophilia. In each one of these courses I have been obliged very frequently to use the term "diathesis," and to justify its use against what I have all along recognized as a widespread and to some extent well-grounded distrust of the vagueness of the knowledge, or, shall I say, of the mere ignorance which its employment not unfrequently denotes. It has thus occurred to me that I could not take for the present course a subject more suitable than the one which I have announced. It will enable me to recapitulate, with amplification, some of the topics to which on former occasions I adverted to briefly, to approach them from a different point of view, and, I trust, to place some of them in a clearer light. In doing this it will be my duty to avoid repetition, but if I should now and then seem to any of my audience who have honored me on former occasions to be attempting to enforce that concerning which I may be thought to have previously said enough, I must beg their indulgence. I must also offer some preliminary apology for the incompleteness and fragmentary character of my lectures. It will be impossible to pass even in the most cursory manner over the whole of the ground indicated, and I shall therefore prefer to dwell with some considerable detail upon certain portions of my subject with which I am personally familiar, and which also appear to have special value as illustrating general laws.

It is needful, in beginning, to define our terms, and in doing this I shall keep as closely as possible to customary usage. We may perhaps define the term *temperament* as applicable to the sum of the physical peculiarities of an individual, exclusive of all definite tendencies to disease. Different temperaments are to be assumed to be likely to give some degree of peculiarity to morbid processes when such have been induced by other causes; but they do not in themselves involve any special proclivity. When most strongly marked, temperament is still consistent with the prolonged enjoyment of perfect health. If there be distinct proclivity, we must then use a stronger term, and speak of *diathesis;* and I would define a diathesis to be any bodily condition, however induced, in virtue of which the individual is, through a long period, or usually through the whole life, prone to suffer from some peculiar type of disease. Some diatheses are inherited, others are acquired. Of some, the effects are permanent or constant; of others, they are transitory, or recurrent after intervals of health. The term should, however, never be applied to any condition of health which is expected to pass away and leave no trace, for the idea of persistency, in some sense, is always implied. On the other hand, we do not confuse diathesis with dyscrasia, for whilst the latter definitely implies bad health, the former only denotes proclivity, and may be used when its subject seems perfectly well. Thus, to distinguish between temperament and diathesis, we may say that the former is a matter of physiology and the latter of disease, and that the former term is applicable only to peculiarities which are a part of the original organization of the individual, whilst the latter may be acquired as well as inherited. Thus, inherited diathesis is more often than not entirely latent at the time of birth, and is susceptible of aggravation, or, in some cases, of cure, in after-life. Such alternations are not possible in the constitutional peculiarities which we name as temperament.

Concerning the term *Idiosyncrasy,* I will not say more in the way of definition than that it is applicable to any definite peculiarity of organization of which the consequences may occur unexpectedly and otherwise inexplicably. It does not, like diathesis, imply any special proneness to disease, only that under certain well-known circumstances results which are peculiar to the individual will certainly occur. Although, as I shall have occasion to observe, it is quite possible that the idiosyncrasies may in many instances have sprung from the diatheses, yet they have become in long hereditary transmissions questions rather of organization than of disease. Their existence may, however, be revealed for the first time at any period of life, and nothing is more common than that an idiosyncrasy should pass into absolute abeyance, to wait until, after it may be a very prolonged period, its proximate exciting cause may again make it conspicuous. Just as observers of mankind have from time to time strained their faculties in the endeavor to find in the external lineaments of a man some clue to his mental power and moral habits, so have physicians sought to find in parallel indications the means of predicting his tendencies in reference to disease. As yet I fear we must say that the labors of the physiognomist and those of the student of temperament have been alike disappointing. Whoever will set himself the task of attempting to classify a given number of individuals according to their temperaments will, I think, soon find himself baffled. He will discover that he is mistaking for criteria of temperament conditions which are simply indicative of youth or age, of health or disease, or the effects of past anxiety or trouble, or of comparative immunity from them. Just as the physiognomist ought carefully to exclude from his estimate of the original and inborn character of a man those traits of expression which have come to him through the wear and tear of life, and keep closely to the original features, so should the student of temperament scrupulously reject all that has been superadded, and which is in a sense accidental. Temperament, as I have endeavored to define it, concerns the original inherited organization of the individual, and does not include anything which is the result of the influences to which his life has exposed him. That which has accrued to him during life goes to produce or aggravate diathesis, but can do nothing in modification of temperament. Dr. Laycock has well spoken of the temperaments as being "fundamental modes of vital activity peculiar to individuals." To some such conception as this we must keep if we would use the word with any precision. Yet a very slight familiarity with the subject will easily show us how difficult it is so to restrict its use, and especially is this the case when dealing with adult and senile periods of life. The very names of the temperaments in many instances denote the record of the results of long-existing disease rather than of individual peculiarities as regards vital activity. Indeed, it may be questioned whether in a large majority of cases there do really exist in persons as yet in perfect health any peculiarities by which we can predicate or discriminate the "fundamental mode of vital activity." Disease, when it occurs, will reveal it to us, and upon this point I shall have much to say in subsequent lectures. But I fear that so long as perfect health exists the data are exceedingly few and un trustworthy. When, for instance, we recognize a melancholic tempera ment, do we not usually take note of something which is the result of disease which has been experienced in the past, rather than of a pecu liarity possessed by the individual whilst in health? The features which go to make up the sanguine temperament, are they not in part, and in large part, often those indicative of sound health in the digestive functions and blood-making organs, and such as might possibly be de stroyed by a few years' illness? If we seek for something more funda mental, shall we not be obliged to confess that we have but little to guide us in a classification excepting the conditions which go to make up what we mean by complexion? In complexion we include the color of the hair and eyes, the state of the skin as regards thickness, thinness, or transparency, and the various degrees of freedom of distribution of blood in the capillaries of the face. It is easy to apply with tolerable accuracy such words as blonde, fair, dark, brunette, sallow, pale, florid, clear, muddy, and the like, and these and many others are epithets ap plicable to the complexion. Temperament, however, although to a large extent confessedly indicated by complexion, is generally held to in clude something more. If it did not I fear we should find it but a sorry basis upon which to build a knowledge of the vital peculiarities of the individual. Yet again, I ask, what have we to which we can make appeal? We may examine a man's features, note the size of his bones, the shape of his jaws, the brilliancy of his eye, the coarseness or fineness of his hair, his stature, his muscularity, his abundance or otherwise of cellular tissue and fat; but in observing all these things we shall be re minded that some of them are simply peculiarities of family or of race, and have little or nothing to do with health, whilst others are condi tions which may vary much at different periods during the same life. Above all, if I mistake not, we shall find it quite impossible to combine with well-known and indelible types of complexion any correlative peculiarities as regards the points which I have just enumerated. We shall find fair persons who have coarse skins, and others of the same tint of hair and eye who have transparent skins. We shall find dark people who are florid, and others who are pale, and we shall have to note that the tendency to fatten varies very much at different periods of life, and that it often depends quite as much upon diet as upon temperament. I come then back to my point, and assert that whoever will set himself to classify by temperament a dozen healthy individuals whom he may chance to meet on a steamboat, in a law court, or at a dinner party, will find that he has scarcely any data excepting those of complexion. He will find, moreover, unless I am much mistaken, that if he attempts to go beyond mere complexion, there are not more than two or three in the dozen whom he can with any degree of confidence assign to special temperaments. As to complexion itself, the further he goes the more he will have to confess that, putting various conditions of sanguification aside as being in many persons dependent upon varying states of health, he can after all classify the complexions themselves only in reference to pigmentation. The varying degrees of dark, fair, or red constitute almost the sole individual peculiarities of the complexion which are not altered by disease or diet.

We come then to the question—Are congenital peculiarities as regards pigmentation in any degree trustworthy as indicative of vital peculiarities in the individual possessing them? We will ask the question first as regards individual races, and next as regards different individuals of the same race. That pigmentation as we now see it in the various races of man is an inherited quality and so definitely transmissible that it constitutes one of the bases of race distinction, may easily be admitted, whilst at the same time we must also grant that it is in itself a result of climate. Those who live in the tropics become dark, without question, as the result of the direct influence of the sun; whilst those who live in more temperate climates lose their pigment, or retain it only in certain special structures, as the hair, the irides, and the choroid. If apparent exceptions to this general law occur, they are to be met with probably as the consequences of human interference in modifying the conditions. Thus, the habit of wearing clothes prevents the development of any approach to blackness of skin in white races who may have lived through many generations in the tropics. The blackest skins always belong to those who have joined the two conditions of nakedness and a tropical sun. Thus, then, to begin at the beginning, may we not believe that varying states of pigmentation of the integument denote rather exposure to climatic influences than peculiarities of development? Nor is there, so far as I know, much reason for believing that variations in this respect imply any material differences in health tendencies. Such peculiarities as we recognize in different races—the immunity of the negro from yellow fever, his liability to elephantiasis and to tetanus—may easily have nothing whatever to do with his pigmentation *per se*, and be matters simply of race. This view, I think, derives considerable support from the facts which I shall mention directly as regards the peculiarities of dark or fair complexions in members of the same race and amongst the lower animals.

If I have seemed to insist too much upon mere differences in complexion as being those to which almost all observers unconsciously trust in their endeavors to discriminate the temperaments in persons in good health, let me ask those who doubt it, to imagine themselves set to classify a group of negroes. It may be that the sameness in negroes is not nearly so great as it may appear to us, who are accustomed to deal with persons of very various types of complexion, and that those who have lived amongst them might be able to effect some sort of classification. We know that in a flock of sheep, which, to the untrained observer, all seem exactly alike, the shepherd can usually find distinctive individual differences. Admitting this, I still doubt, however, whether it would be practicable to apply to a race, in which all the individuals are highly pigmented, many of the facts which have hitherto been held to discriminate temperaments. We can recognize easily individual peculiarities—we can recognize also the peculiarities of race—but if the race be pure and the color uniform, we should have remarkably little to guide us. This statement leads obviously to the suggestion that I am perhaps involving myself in a fallacy, and that it may be the fact that what have been called the temperaments are observed almost solely under conditions in which the race is much mixed. It is certainly true that doctrines on this subject have been developed only under conditions of long-established civilization, and where the population represented those who derived their blood from various sources. Dr. Laycock has given a valuable hint in this direction, and has remarked that we greatly need a British ethnology founded on well-defined and distinct characteristics. Thus, it might be, perhaps, much nearer the truth if we were to classify those who make up our own population not according to complexion, as fair, red, black, etc., nor by reference to certain more or less hypothetical vital tendencies, as lymphatic, bilious, sanguine, phlegmatic, and the like, but rather as Celtic, Scandinavian, Roman, or English. It is quite true that we should find a comparatively small number who could be definitely placed under any one of these heads, and that the large majority present features of racial mixture which would utterly defy classification. But the same difficulty has to be met by those who prefer to make groups under the head of temperament. A large majority belong to no one in particular, and partake of the characteristics of several at once. Modern historical authorities are desirous, I am aware, to have it believed that the English population is not mixed to anything like the extent which it was formerly the custom to suppose. They delight to claim us as *English* pure and simple, and to mean by the term direct pure-blooded descendants of the Angles and the Saxons. They appeal to the fact of what is called the Saxon invasion—I must ask pardon, the *English* invasion—as to the entire extermination of the Romanized British population, from the land of which we are now in possession. They appeal also, and I must admit with more cogency, to the almost absolute substitution of a German language for the British tongue. There are, however, I think, good reasons why the student of race and believers in its permanency should hesitate to accept fully this new creed. We have amongst us far too many who possess not only typical Roman noses, but all the peculiarities of character which usually accompany the Roman cast of face. It is more difficult to feel certain as to the persistency of the British or Celtic element, since we know much less well what its peculiarities were. Whatever the evidence may be as to extermination by the invaders of the males who opposed them, nothing is less probable than that the women were included in the massacre. An army of invading and colonizing males would be certain to preserve sufficiently numerous representatives of the conquered race to effect a very material modification of the future stock. Whilst on this subject it is also, I think, fair to suggest that the present frequency of the Roman face in England, may not improbably be due in part to prepotency in that remarkable race.

Although I would by no means propose classification by race as likely to be of any great value in reference to clinical research, yet I do seriously think that it would be more practicable, and come nearer to the truth, than the classification by temperament. A glance at what has been attempted in the latter direction will, I think, convince us that even those who manifested the greatest ingenuity, and possessed the soundest and most extensive knowledge concerning health and disease, have been obliged, when describing the temperaments, to avail themselves of many criteria which are really the phenomena of disease. Chief among those to whom I allude stands one to whom I have myself been greatly indebted—my first teacher of medicine, the late Professor Laycock. With a power of insight which amounted almost to genius, Dr. Laycock had applied his mind to the study of the physiognomical diagnosis of disease, and by long practice in observations in this direction, he was enabled sometimes to give opinions which astonished those who were accustomed to more plodding methods of investigation. In a series of lectures delivered in 1861, and published in the following year in the ' Medical Times and Gazette,' he embodied the results of his experience. He believed that his rules of diagnosis were to a large extent based upon peculiarities of temperament, and he naturally gave great attention to the correct classification of these so-called fundamental states. For myself, I cannot doubt that the knowledge which he found so useful was based not so much on the discrimination of temperaments as on the recognition of diathesis. I could illustrate this statement by innumerable quotations from the lectures to which I have referred, in which features distinctly the result of bygone disease are mentioned, as if they formed part of the original organization. Our time will not permit that I should enter into any detail upon this point; but as Dr. Laycock's is, so far as I know, the last and certainly by far the best of all attempts to classify temperaments, I think it may be convenient that we should devote a few minutes to its consideration. He endeavored, as he tells us, to avoid the use of new terms, and to apply the old ones with definite meaning, as significant of predominant modes of vital activity. He recognized six divisions—first, persons nervously active from predominant innervation; secondly, those with predominant sanguification and activity of the vascular and muscular systems; thirdly, those in whom both innervation and muscular activity are predominant, and this existing with also predominant carbon deposit or excretion—*the fibrous or bilious temperament;* fourthly, when the muscular system is well developed, but neither sanguification nor innervation predominant, and there is a decided tendency to the deposit of fat—*the phlegmatic temperament;* fifthly, those who are defective as regards innervation, sanguification, and muscular and vascular activity—*the lymphatic temperament;* and, sixthly, those in whom, with defective innervation, sanguification, and vascular activity, there is a combined tendency to carbon deposit—*the melancholic temperament.* Here we have, with a little expansion, the original four temperaments—sanguine, nervous, bilious, and lymphatic. Let us ask if they are real, and if the features by which they are to be recognized are such as are likely to be permanent in the individual, and unmodified by alterations in his state of health. In the first place, I would suggest that the melancholic temperament and the bilious temperament are, after all, only different degrees of the same thing, and that, as life advances, the one is very apt to pass into the other; and, further, that the distinguishing feature in both is one which concerns disease rather than temperament, and which might be more conveniently known as the hepatic *diathesis.* It is the proneness to disordered function on the part of the liver, its ready and frequent occurrence, which for the most part stamps peculiarity on both these so-called temperaments. Further, it is much to be doubted whether this facility of hepatic disturbance would be found in association exclusively, or even generally, with any particular cast of the features, or, recognizable peculiarities in the general frame. Certainly it is not, by any means, the exclusive possession of dark complexioned persons, nor, perhaps, does it more abound amongst dark complexioned nations—the Italians, to wit—than amongst others. It is a matter of race, of family, and of climate. It may be diminished or aggravated by various conditions of life, and it is usually recognizable only after certain definite phenomena of disease have been already experienced. As regards its being worth while to distinguish any condition as the nervous temperament because innervation is predominant—or, in other words, the central cerebro-spinal system is largely developed—much doubt may, I think, reasonably be felt. A high development of the nervous system is again a peculiarity of race and of family rather than of anything with which we as medical observers have to do. The conditions in which the nervous system is subject to disease are rather those of instability than of simple preponderance. The phlegmatic temperament gets its peculiarity from the tendency to fatten; but, as I have already observed, this tendency is shown in different periods of life, and is much modified by habits of diet and social surroundings. So of the lymphatic temperament, in which all functions are sluggish, and a general failure of what we may call "tone" is the conspicuous peculiarity. I would submit that this condition is not unfrequently induced by disease occurring during the lifetime of the individual, and not by anything which can possibly be denoted by peculiarities in the general formation. Dr. Laycock's classification of the temperaments is also, in common with the older ones, open to the criticism that, inasmuch as it takes little or no account of the more conspicuous differences in complexion, it affords us but few facts by which to recognize them. When a man is florid and muscular, it is not difficult to say that he is of the sanguine temperament; but these conditions are, perhaps, indicative rather of good digestion and sound health than of intrinsic peculiarities. The appetite may fail, or the health give way, and some of the signs supposed to denote temperament may easily vanish. Would it not be more convenient to speak of a man as being simply, for the time being, florid and muscular, than by the use of such a term as "sanguine temperament" to imply permanency in qualities which may easily prove to be otherwise? If we cannot identify the sanguine temperament by other characters, probably it would. The peculiarities which denote family and race must be viewed with the utmost caution, as well by the physiognomist in reference to character as by the physician in respect to tendencies to disease. They are usually of no use, and they may easily mislead. It is only indirectly that they may become valuable—that is, when the special proclivities of the race or family in question are known beforehand. A thick upper lip, when it occurs in a mulatto, denotes descent only, and not scrofula. The peculiarities of the Hebrew features reveal only the race, and are of use to the physician only so far as he may be acquainted with the facts as to the special tendencies to disease in that race.

I have been speaking thus far on the subject of temperament considered as the aggregate of a man's physical personality, and have felt obliged to return the verdict that its study in this form is but little useful for our purposes as surgeons. It will I think, however, be well to say a few additional words respecting some of the individual peculiarities which have been held to make up temperament.

We will begin with the subject of *complexion*. The color of the hair, skin, and eyes may be easily observed, and although the English population, in a majority of cases, is a very mixed one, yet abundant opportunities occur of taking note of very definite types. Observations are yet wanting which would justify us in believing that any special tendencies to disease are implied by differences in the pigmentation of the hair and skin. It is, however, a subject of much interest for further research, and thinking that it might possibly be useful to others, I have placed before you a brief list of the more definite complexions which I prepared for my own guidance many years ago when investigating the subject of scrofula. In endeavoring to determine whether any given disease occurs in special connection with any one complexion, we are met at once with the difficulty that we do not know what the relative proportions of the several complexions are in the English population. Nor would it be sufficiently accurate for the purposes of any local observer to know the proportions of fair, rufous, dark, etc., in the British population generally, since these probably vary very considerably in different districts, and even in different towns. I cannot but think that careful statistics upon this head—collected in small towns and villages where it might be practicable to count the whole, and made, too, by trained observers—would prove of considerable value in more than one direction. It is in external diseases chiefly, such as lupus, psoriasis, and the like, of which the diagnosis is easy, that we should find the best opportunities for testing prevalence in relation to complexion. At one time I had formed a strong opinion that lupus, to take a marked example, was met with much more frequently in those of dark complexions, persons of dark brown hair, brown eyes, and a bluish sclerotic through which the pigment of the choroid is somewhat seen. I have collected a good deal of statistical evidence on this point, but it remains useless so long as we are ignorant of the relative proportions of the complexions amongst those from whom the cases came. It is probably the fact that both professional and lay observations concur in supporting the creed, that there are differences—mental, moral, and physical—between the fair and the dark; yet it would be exceedingly difficult to say anything definite as to what these differences are. I was myself taught by a careful practical observer, the late Mr. Wormald, that all persons of the dark complexion would bear mercurial treatment well, and would require larger doses than those who are fair. I have been accustomed ever since to act on this belief, and I think it is certainly well founded, although there are many exceptions to it. I have even gone farther than my teacher and come to believe that a great many persons of the dark complexion not only bear mercury well, but enjoy better health whilst taking it, and are not unfrequently much and permanently benefited by a long course. It is but fair that I should admit, however, that one of the most remarkable examples of tolerance of this drug which I have ever met with, occurred in a patient of very fair complexion. Further, I have acquired, possibly on insufficient data, a sort of practical belief to the effect that dark-complexioned persons do not bear direct tonics well, that the need of purgatives is greater in them, and that they are often not helped by sea-air. Beyond these items of uncertain creed I cannot go, and even granting that they are sound, it remains still an open question whether the mere difference in pigmentation is, *per se*, their explanation. It may be after all that this difference in complexion is, as we see it in English society, mainly useful as a clue to descent, to family, and remotely to race. Many facts concur to imply this. When an albino chances to occur in a dark family (as is usual), he does not, I believe, show any special liabilities to disease, or differ in any way from his brothers and sisters, excepting in the local inconvenience as regards eyes and skin. White horses, white cattle, white rabbits, and white poultry are usually not possessed of any other correlative peculiarities. There is a prejudice, and probably it is nothing better, that they are slightly more delicate than colored animals. The breed of pigs in the South of England is usually black, whilst in the northern counties white-skinned pigs are universally preferred. Such a fact is conclusive in proof that mere difference in pigmentation of the skin makes no material difference as to health or feeding capabilities. In the different breeds of sheep we have frequent illustrations of the power of race and family in giving peculiarity as regards the tolerance of climate and proclivity to some diseases. But the occurrence of a pigmented animal in any given breed does not, as far as I am aware, entail any difference as regards health. The only observation with which I am acquainted which contravenes this statement is one quoted by Mr. Darwin, to the effect that black sheep can eat with impunity a certain species of *Hypericum*, which is poisonous to white ones. This observation is so peculiar and so isolated that it must be held to require further confirmation. Possibly, the strongest instance in illustration of the unimportance of difference in general pigmentation occurs in the case of the common ferret. These animals breed albinos very readily, and probably three fourths of those at present in use in England have red eyes and white hair, the remaining quarter being of a dark brown color. So far as I know, the one is just as hardy as the other, and they are fed and treated in every way alike. Thus, then, I think we may believe that in the English climate the abundance or comparative absence of pigment in the tissues does not, *per se*, make any appreciable difference in the vital endowments of the individual. I am far from wishing to imply in saying this that the study of the complexions, as regards pigment, is useless for clinical purposes. Its uses have, however, for the most part, yet to be discovered, and it is desirable to note, in passing, that although we name the complexions chiefly in reference to pigmentation, something more than simply abundance or deficiency is to be recognized in them. Thus, the rufous complexion is due not merely to deficiency, but to peculiarity in quality, and is probably usually the result of the mixture of dissimilars. It is very likely that a careful observation of a larger number of rufous persons would confirm the popular belief that they do display peculiarities, not only in temper and general character, but to a certain extent as regards proclivity to disease. Again, the occurrence of great differences in color between the eyes and the hair, the eyes being much lighter than the hair—as, for instance, black hair with blue eyes—is probably an indication of delicacy. This, at any rate, is the general belief.

Next in importance to the differences in pigmentation we have certain other conditions which are usually included in what is meant by complexion, such as the thickness or thinness of skin, its transparency, the development of its glandular system, and the state of its appendages. I dare not venture to say more respecting most of these than that they are well worthy of further observation. We have exceedingly little definite information regarding the clinical value of any of them. We know that thick, coarse skins are more liable to be attacked by acne than are those which are thinner; or, rather, perhaps I ought to say that acne assumes different forms in relation to the original endowments of the skin which it attacks. In those of coarse skins comedones, papules, and pustules easily form, or we may even have a condition of tuberous hypertrophy, whilst in those of thin, transparent skins, if the causes of acne come into operation, an erythematous condition will be produced, and the term *rosacea* become applicable. We believe—I scarcely dare say that we know—that in children in whom the hairs are thick and coarse the ringworm fungus finds an uncongenial home. It might be possible to mention a few other detached observations as to certain peculiarities in the skin and its appendages, not themselves due to disease, which may guide us in estimating the future liabilities of the individual. As a matter of general observation it may be asserted that all marked deviations from the normal type should be held in some degree of suspicion. Thus, if the hair is markedly coarse, or unusually fine, if the skin be very thick or very transparent, we are perhaps justified in suspecting that there may be in other tissues similar departures from the average constitution, some of which may prove inconsistent with the preservation of perfect health. For the present, however, it is speculation only. Of accurate observations we have none. The teeth and the nails may be suitably mentioned together as structures in which we very frequently observe with great interest and profit the indelible consequences of past disease. These, however, belong to the subject of diathesis, and do not concern us now. As regards peculiarities of these structures occurring quite independently of previous disease, our knowledge is much in the same state as on the subject to which I have just referred. Peculiarities in the form of the teeth are often matters of family descent, and teach us nothing as regards their possessor's liabilities. It is probable, however, that all peculiarities as regards color and texture of teeth are of value, in proportion as they

depart from the normal standard, as indicative of defective tissue formation in general.   Dr. Laycock, in the interesting lectures to which I
have alluded, has examined at much length the various conditions of
the Ear as indicative of temperament and diathesis.   He believed that
the form of the ear was of great value as a clue to the original development of the brain, and that the state of its nutrition, blood supply,
etc., might help us to estimate corresponding conditions within the
cranium.   His conclusions in the main are probably correct, but we
may doubt whether he did not push matters too far in assigning a
special state of ear to such conditions as general paralysis, and in con-
sidering in reference to this disease that the congenital adhesion of the
lobule to the cheek had some degree of significance.   His observations
had led him greatly to prefer ears which had free lobules, and these,
too, of considerable size, which had all their different parts well marked,
and which were moderately fleshy, not thin and cartilaginous.   As regards the matter of the lobule, it may be plausibly suggested that its
adhesion or otherwise indicates only family descent, and implies nothing
as to temperament, and the same to some extent is probably true as
regards the state of the helix and other parts.   Making allowance,
however, for sources of fallacy in these directions, I think there can be
no doubt that the different states of the ear, as well congenital as acquired, have been unduly neglected both by the physiognomist and the
physician.   The ear affords excellent facilities for observation as to the
general state of nutrition and circulation, and the degree of perfection
in its form is a tolerably safe guide as to the descent of the individual
from a sound and well-bred stock.   That it furnishes a clue to the
state of circulation in the brain better than does the color of the cheeks
and nose, or anything like as good as that afforded by the brightness of
the eyes, may be doubted, and before we make inferences on this point,
we must remember that the ears, as well as the nose, are remarkably
exposed to the influence of external temperature.

I have said so much in disparagement as well of the general as of the
special signs which have been held to indicate temperament, that I fear
it may be suspected that I almost doubt the reality of temperament in
itself.   If I have given that impression let me hasten at once to remove
it.   There can be no question whatever as to the reality of the differ-

ence between individuals, nor any doubt as to the importance of the recognition of those differences by the medical practitioner. By far the commonest error of the prescriber, and one which most interferes with his success, is the easy-going habit of regarding all persons as alike, and recognizing differences only in their diseases; or, to put it in other language, of ignoring the predisposing causes, and taking account only of immediate ones. The farmer who would succeed in his pursuits must not content himself with making sure that he has sown good seed, and according to the most approved methods. He must go further back to take knowledge of the nature of the soil with which he has to deal, of the crops which it has previously borne, and of the manures which have been used. It is much the same with us in the diagnosis and treatment of disease. In addition to the primary or exciting cause, which is of paramount importance, we have various others which may perhaps be conveniently classed together under the term *contributory*, since they contribute to control and modify final results. Amongst these temperament—the original vital endowment of the individual—is unquestionably a real force, and one which we would most gladly recognize and estimate if we could. The scepticism which I have been expressing applies not to the reality of the thing, but to our ability to discriminate it. I shall have to speak in my next lecture on the subject of idiosyncrasy, and one of the facts which I think will come before us in the clearest possible light is, that we possess no means whatever of recognizing by external configuration the subjects of these remarkable deviations from the normal state. Who shall discover beforehand the subject of hay asthma or the man in whom the iodide of potassium will act like a poison? When I come to the subject of diathesis we shall be on wholly different and far firmer ground. Defining diathesis as a persisting morbid proclivity we shall be able to show that in a great many instances, either by the aspect of the individual, or the history of the case, a clear and definite opinion can be arrived at. The differences which have been held to constitute temperament have had their remote origin in two sources of influence; first, the hereditary transmission of the peculiarities incident to race and family, which, for the most part, entail no morbid proclivity whatever; and, secondly, to some one or more of the various common causes of disease acting, perhaps, through

2

many generations.   Thus, I cannot but think that what has been called temperament divides itself naturally into these two parts, *race* and *diathesis*.   There is therefore but little advantage in retaining the word, more especially when we have regard to the inextricable complexity of the subject.   As regards diathesis, the conditions are very different. We can study the results of different causes in detail and with much precision; we can express our knowledge in clear terms, and recognizing the fact that we frequently-encounter several of these causes in activity together, we can investigate with interest the mixed forms of diathesis which result.   We do not embarrass ourselves by admitting extraneous complications based on the peculiarities of race.   Making due allowance for acclimatization, we assert that, within certain limits,—not wholly unimportant, but relatively very much so—the various causes of disease act in the same way on individuals of very different races.   It is in this direction, if I am not mistaken, that the work of the future will be done.   We shall see that the connection between special diseases and the external configuration of the body is less close than has been assumed, and that the best plan is to study carefully the scope of power of each kind of morbid influence under the varied circumstances which may attend its action.

Dr. W. E. Waters,
U. S. ARMY.

LECTURE II.

MR. PRESIDENT AND GENTLEMEN,—We concern ourselves to-day with some of the most remarkable facts in respect to what is known as *Idiosyncrasy*. In the definitions which were attempted in the previous lecture it was fully admitted, nay insisted on, that this word is intended to denote our ignorance of causes, though in no degree to express disbelief in their existence. Probably this ignorance will be, in most instances, only temporary, and the results which we need assign to idiosyncrasy and leave thus unexplained will, one by one, be transferred to the domain of the several diatheses concerning the causes of which something, at any rate, if not all, is known. Idiosyncrasy is, indeed, to a large extent, nothing but diathesis brought to a point. It is peculiarity of constitution in some one particular feature developed to a height which at first sight seems inexplicable and possibly almost absurd. It is individuality run mad. In seeking to understand the real nature of that with which under this name we have to deal, we must keep in mind that it is by no means always the isolated phenomenon which at first sight it appears. For one man who rises to the height of peculiarity which deserves the name *miser*, there are a thousand in whom the quality of thriftiness is developed in various degrees beyond what is praiseworthy. The miser is only the thrifty man developed in great excess. So it is with the relations between diathesis and idiosyncrasy; for one person who cannot take the smallest dose of quinine there are thousands who betray unusual susceptibility to the drug, and many of them in high degrees. Here, I think, we gain an insight into the way in which idiosyncrasies possibly take their origin. They are diatheses, or parts of diatheses, developed, intensified, and specialized by hereditary transmission. That they depend upon structural peculiarities we cannot doubt, although we may be quite unable to demonstrate their physical cause. The man who is poisoned by a drop of atropine solution

19

applied to his conjunctiva is as certainly the subject of some peculiarity in his nervous organization as are those who cannot distinguish red from green, or those who are born without the sense of hearing.

It may here be remarked that the term idiosyncrasy is not, I think, ever applied to acquired peculiarities, but solely to those that are congenital. Some, perhaps, may be overcome; many, as age advances, undergo modification, but, as a rule, all are present at birth, and persist through the whole of life. It is probable that all, when once developed, are hereditarily transmissible, and I am obliged to believe strongly that if inquiry were made we should, in almost all instances, find that all strongly-marked idiosyncrasies had been present in some degree in former generations. I suggested in last year's lectures, and with, I think, much plausibility, that the hæmorrhagic diathesis—so strongly hereditary when once produced, unknown in the lower animals, and frequently coincident in the individual with gout—has its origin in the peculiarities of vascular structure which are developed by gout, and which have become modified and specialized by transmission through many generations. So I would venture now to ask consideration for similar hypotheses in reference to the other forms of idiosyncrasy of most, or of all, of which every fragment of genealogy has been lost.

We have defined idiosyncrasy to be a peculiarity of the individual, usually a rare and exceptional one, which does not necessarily entail any degree of proclivity to disease, but which may become obvious under a variety of exciting causes. It is often much as if by the introduction of some test solution, a chemist should discover the presence of chloride of sodium, or some other salt, in water which he had had no reason previously to suspect. The various incidents of life in connection with diet, drugs, and the exposure to the ordinary causes of disease, apply these tests for us, and most unexpected revelations do they sometimes make. We find that an individual apparently in no respect different from those around him, is poisoned by the smallest quantity of some ordinary drug, or that he cannot digest some one article of diet which is daily food to his companions; or, again, that the virus of some specific fever either produces on him no apparent effect, or may be attended by symptoms of tenfold their usual violence. Sometimes it is an extraordinary immunity which is revealed, and sometimes an almost incredible degree of susceptibility.

We can never predicate anything as regards idiosyncrasies of function until the trial has been made. There are, however, a certain class of individual peculiarities of the same nature which do not always remain concealed. I allude to those in which the structure of some external and visible organ is affected. The peculiarities which we have hitherto classed as idiosyncrasies concern function only. But a moment's consideration will make it evident that they must depend on structure, and that they have really exact parallels in certain congenital defects or peculiarities in external organization, which may or may not entail inconvenience to the individual. A coloboma of the iris is a structural idiosyncrasy, so also is the persistence of the nerve sheath in the retinal nerve fibres in the human eye, which the ophthalmoscope occasionally reveals. And each of these peculiarities may, indeed, must, entail some degree of deviation from the normal condition of vision. It is true that some congenital defects of structure occur in such an irregular manner that we prefer rather to class them, at any rate for the present, as mere accidents of development, or freaks of nature, than as idiosyncrasies, such are, for instance, moles, nævi, and the like. In the idiosyncrasies, however marvellous some of them may be, there is usually to be noticed a certain reference to law and order. They do not occur absolutely by chance, and they often appear to be correlated with other less startling peculiarities, and they often happen to several members of the same family, or are distinctly hereditary. I have instanced coloboma of the iris as an example of congenital idiosyncrasy of structure, and by its side I might put hare-lip, clefts in the eyelid, absence of the levator palpebræ, and many similar defects.

These congenital peculiarities of structure which do not entail any tendency to advancing disease of the whole organization, but remain permanently local, and must, therefore, rank as idiosyn rasies rather than diatheses, are not always apparent at the time of birth. Thus, a child may be born with its skin, so far as can be observed, in a healthy condition, but in whom within a few months of birth a harshness will be noticed which will steadily develop itself into the typical condition of ichthyosis. If this happened to but a single child in a family we might search about for some cause of disease to which the infant had been subjected. But, if it happens to child after child in the same family, we cease our quest in this direction, and begin to feel certain that it must depend upon some congenital peculiarity in the structure of the skin itself.

Permit me next to ask your attention in some little detail to two groups of facts recently brought under my notice which will illustrate my argument. Mr. Balmanno Squire was kind enough last autumn to bring for my inspection a series of cases of most unusual interest. Very briefly the facts were these. Three children from the country, two sisters and a brother, of apparently healthy parentage, and having several other brothers and sisters who ailed nothing, were themselves the subjects of a malady the precise counterpart of which I had never seen before. It was exactly alike, with some minor differences of degree, in all the three children. Had it been a congenital deformity or arrest of development, its occurrence in several members of the same family would have been nothing remarkable, and we should have been able to place it, without any fresh wonderment at the marvels of pathogenesis, by the side of ichthyosis, color-blindness, deaf-mutism, and other well-recognized family diseases. But the malady in question by no means fitted closely with these. It had not been congenital in any one instance, but had developed in each child some years after birth. It consisted in an inflammation of the skin of the face and upper extremities, which had covered them with crusts and scabs, and which on some parts of the face, the nose especially, had caused ulcerations exactly like lupus. In fact, any one seeing the nose only would have had no hesitation in naming the disease lupus. But on the arms it was different. Here there was no evidence of new growth and very little of ulceration, but simply a diffuse, more or less pustular inflammation. From the occurrence of the disease on those parts most exposed to the air it was to be assumed that such exposure was the exciting cause. As it had not materially varied with season, and as the feet had not suffered from chilblains, we may conjecture that the irritating influences were wind and sun rather than direct cold. Let it be noted that in each of these three cases the disease had persisted for several years, and, allow me to repeat, that in all three children it was essentially alike.

What a lesson have we here as to the possibilities of hereditary dia-thetic proclivity! It may easily be the fact that not in the whole population of the British Isles, at the present moment, another case could be found which should offer anything approaching at all closely the disease I have described; and yet it had been possible, in the cases of three children, for the influence of parental combination of tendencies, to be so definite and so peculiar, that they all developed it in precisely the same form. I have already mentioned ichthyosis as affording us an example of a disease which is often met with unexpectedly in many members of the same family, and probably, after all, it affords us the nearest parallel which we can find to these cases. It, however, in greater or less degree, is tolerably common, and generally there is some history of its having happened in former generations. It, too, is very often congenital, or if not actually present at the time of birth, it develops so soon afterwards, that we can easily believe that at any rate the peculiarity of skin giving tendency to it was congenital, and was of the nature of an arrest in the perfection of development. In the cases which I have described, however, the mind less easily grasps such an hypothesis, the disease being distinctly of an inflammatory kind, not affecting the whole surface, and not beginning until a considerable period after birth. Ichthyosis, for the most part, appears to be independent of local exciting causes, though it is by no means wholly so; and we must re-member that in Mr. Squire's cases, although local causes are clearly influ-ential, they have been so trivial in amount that we are obliged to place the inherited proclivities of the tissue in by far the foremost position.

Inherited proclivity of tissue of a similar kind, that is giving tendency at a certain age, under very insignificant exciting causes, to definite and peculiar forms of inflammation is probably a thing which we very fre-quently encounter in practice, but it is not often that we can demon-strate its reality in such a striking manner as Mr. Squire's series of cases enables us to do. It is chiefly on this account, although in itself an extreme rarity, yet teaching us a wide lesson, that I have thought it worth your attention. When we see tubercular disease of the lungs manifest itself in one after the other of a number of brothers and sisters without obvious cause and run its course in each unchecked by treat-ment, we probably witness an illustration of the same pathological law.

It is to be remembered further that, although it is only when several members of the same family show tendency under the same circumstances to disease of the same part that the doctrine of inherited proclivity of tissue is strongly enforced, there is yet every reason to believe that the same cause is operative in countless examples of disease occurring only in single individuals. During the winter session just past two series of remarkable examples of xanthelasma in children, and in several members of the same family at the same age, have been brought before the Pathological Society. In one of these two brothers and a sister, now adults, were shown by Dr. Stephen Mackenzie, all three the subjects of xanthelasma in a slight but definite form, and all with the history that it had been noticed at birth. Mr. James Startin showed a brother and sister, still young children, in whom similar conditions were present in much more conspicuous forms, and in whom they had been noticed within a few years of birth, but were believed not to be congenital. In all these cases the changes are symmetrical, and occur in the limbs, neck, and trunk, omitting that part most usually affected when the disease develops, *de novo*, in adults, namely, the eyelids. In none is the affection attended by any derangement of general health, or tendency to liver disorder, and it seems probable from Dr. Mackenzie's cases that there is no tendency to increase, the three patients, now adults, having been in their present condition from early childhood. Thus, the general features of the malady differ exceedingly from those of the more common form as we see it in adults, and approach those of some other forms of skin disease—psoriasis and ichthyosis, for example. Histologically, however, the local changes in those cases are those of xanthelasma, and as such we must class them. In Mr. Startin's case the resemblance to psoriasis, as regards symmetry and location of patches on the tips of the elbows, etc., was very marked.

If speculation respecting such rare conditions may be permitted, I think it should proceed somewhat on these lines. We know, respecting psoriasis, that it is very hereditary, persisting through many generations, but rarely showing itself in more than a single member of the same family, and not unfrequently undergoing apparent transmutation into other forms of skin disease, as, for instance, nummular eczema, lichen ruber, pemphigus, and ichthyosis.

Of its connection with the latter malady—parents the subject of psoriasis having ichthyotic children—I adduced some evidence in my last year's course of lectures. Of ichthyosis itself we know that it usually occurs in several members of the same family, is hereditary, but often omits a generation, or fails to descend in the direct line. Xanthelasma we have as yet known only as a disease which occurs chiefly on the eyelids of adults who have suffered from liver disorder, and which hardly ever in adults develops on other parts of the skin, excepting when in connection with jaundice. It is in part a new growth, and in part a fatty degeneration, and its peculiarities as regards color, etc., clearly have a close connection with the presence of bile pigments in the blood. I do not think that there can be much dispute as to the possibility of inheritance of any tendency to tissue change which has existed for a long time in the individual who was its first subject, and in whom it had showed itself a considerable time before the birth of offspring. Nor is it in the least certain, perhaps not even probable, that such hereditary tendency would be manifested in the first generation. If we apply these facts to the explanation of the occurrence of xanthelasma as a family, and almost as a congenital disease, apparently of no diathetic significance, I think we should conjecture that it is probably derived from some progenitor who had acquired the ordinary hepatic form of adults. And further, I cannot help the suggestion that it is possible that this inheritance has met and combined with a degree of proclivity to that group of skin diseases of which psoriasis is the best type.

Let me recapitulate: If a child shows within a year or two of birth yellow tubercles on its elbows, and delicate yellow streaks and spots in the flexures of the hips and popliteal spaces, exactly such as we are familiar with in connection with severe jaundice in the adult, and with jaundice only, we at first seek for evidence of disease of the liver. But if we find similar conditions produced at about the same age in two or three members of the same family, and the same series of events happening in more than one family, we again, as in the case of ichthyosis, cease our search for the ordinary causes of the disease, and fall back upon the hypothesis of what I have ventured to term structural idiosyncrasy. We feel sure that the skin of the parts affected must have been at birth in a state of peculiarity, although we failed to be able to prove

it.   It is, of course, possible that the congenital peculiarity was not in
the skin alone.   It may have been in the blood also; but if we observe,
in the subsequent life of the patient, that the peculiar conditions remain
restricted to the parts first affected, that they have no aggressive power,
and that the general health of the individual does not suffer in the least,
our first impression as to the idiosyncrasy being purely one of local
structure becomes revived and strengthened.

I am yet very anxious to make clear the argument that congenital
structural peculiarity may entail liability to local disease, and that such
disease may be locally aggressive—at any rate, for a certain time, perhaps
indefinitely—because I think it is one which may, probably, explain a
large class of pathological facts, some of which are of a far less definite
character than those to which we have just referred.   Let us use icthy-
osis and xanthelasma of young children as definite and palpable illustrations of what is possible, although admittedly rare, and guided by the
light which we obtain from their investigation, let us examine the facts
as to some other much less definite maladies.   In the condition known
as molluscum fibrosum, little tumors—possibly fibro-cellular, possibly
glandular—develop in or under the skin.   Usually there are very few
of them, and examples of the malady, when only two, three, or half-a-
dozen are present, are very common.   In rare cases, however, the whole
surface is affected, and the tumors may be counted by hundreds, or even
thousands.   The tendency to their production may be noticed for the
first time at almost any period of life, but if they are to be numerous, it
begins almost invariably in early childhood.   Whether there be many,
or whether there be few, the general health remains good, and there is
no evidence whatever of any correlated tendency to general disease.   Is
it not very probable that the liability to molluscum fibrosum is inbred
in the original development of the integument, that we are witnessing
the results of an idiosyncrasy of structure?   Let us see how the matter
stands as regards common psoriasis.   In this instance we have no new
growth of tumors, but only a tendency on the part of special regions of
the skin, possibly of almost the whole of it, to take on a certain peculiar
type of chronic inflammation.   This tendency occurs in its best marked
forms, and most frequently to young persons, although, let us note, it
is never congenital, and never even infantile.   It is never associated

with anything that we can appreciate as ill-health, and the facts with which we are acquainted as regards the conditions which may influence it for the worse, are few and insignificant. Excepting so far as it may be supposed to act by interfering with the functions of the skin, it does not produce any derangement of the patient's health. It is hereditary, but not prone to prevail in many members of a single family. Is it not probable that a disease, of which these statements are true, is one not originally or wholly due either to the blood or to the nervous system, but in large, and chief part, to an idiosyncrasy in the structure of the skin? In proportion as the disease is late in its development—in other words, in proportion as we find it apparently waiting for the exciting influence to assist its birth—may we assume the probability that the idiosyncrasy is less strong. The explanation of the entire absence of psoriasis in infancy and early childhood may possibly be found in the suggestion that, when the structural idiosyncrasy is very strong, it manifests itself in a different form. Thus, I think it not improbable that ichthyosis of infants may be in this way the representative of the psoriasis tendency in its intensest form. I must not weary you in arguing the case in reference to other diseases of the skin, or of other parts, but simply state that whenever we find a strictly local malady which develops itself in all instances with little or no apparent cause, is hereditary, is but little aggressive, and only in a sort of accidental way influences the health of its subject, we are entitled to suspect structural idiosyncrasy. Steatomata on the scalp, lipomata, adenomatous tumors in the breast, multiple uterine fibroids, milinm, whether on the face or elsewhere, and a host of others, are probably examples of what I have tried to describe. From these it needs but little ingenuity to perceive that it is only a matter of degree if we should pass to the development of new growths in general, both malignant and innocent, and to many disorders which do not fit at all exactly with the description which I have given and concerning which we can say a good deal as to our knowledge of their exciting causes. In a multitude of these, hereditary, but wholly latent, peculiarity of structure may not improbably take its share in the production of the special result. They are examples of what may be termed complicated or conditional idiosyncrasy.

I must hasten to other departments of our subject. As surgeons we

have to encounter the results of functional idiosyncrasy chiefly in reference to drugs and the specific fevers. The department of diet I ought,
perhaps, to leave to physicians, yet it is impossible that I should wholly
do so. For the patients who consult us about other maladies will often
describe to us symptoms which we should wholly misinterpret were we
not familiar with what is possible in reference to diet idiosyncrasy. A
few years ago it fell to my lot to become much interested in the subject
of idiosyncrasy as regards eggs. Several patients consulted me within a
short period, who, amongst other symptoms, described a liability to
attacks of violent vomiting, or of a sense of sinking and abdominal distress which were to them inexplicable. In more than one of these the
reason of my being consulted was that the attacks were attended by
temporary defect in sight. In one instance the patient was an artist,
who declared that frequently he was quite unable, for several hours at
a time, to see to paint. His defect seemed to be a temporary suspension of the power of accommodation. It always affected both eyes, and
was always attended by a sense of heat at the stomach and abdominal
discomfort. I found that these attack usually occurred within an hour
or two of breakfast, and on entering into detail I became convinced
that they were due to eating eggs. On telling my patient my conclusion
he replied at once that he had always suspected it, yet being very fond
of eggs, he had indulged in one once in a month or so. He was quite
cured by abstinence. In several of the cases to which I refer, the
symptoms produced were far more violent than in this one, and had
been so severe on some occasions as to lead to the suspicion that poison
had been given. In some cases susceptibility as regards eggs is observed
in reference to all eggs, and in all conditions as regards freshness, and
in respect also to the very smallest quantity, so that a little egg taken in
a pudding, a sauce, or a soup, may produce the most definite disagreement. In some the susceptibility is invariable, but in others it may be
much diminished, or entirely removed when its subject is in unusually
good health, or taking much exercise in the open air. In many instances the liability to egg-poisoning is manifested only in respect to the
eggs of certain birds, or eggs under certain special conditions as regards
cookery or keeping. Eggs and fish, the two articles of diet respecting
which most is to be said as regards peculiar susceptibilities, are, it is to

be remembered, the two which are most easily capable of peculiar changes from over-keeping. A fish which is quite wholesome when absolutely fresh may become exceedingly otherwise if kept only for a few hours after death, a fact with which those who live in hot countries are abundantly familiar. The same is true, though to a less extent, in respect to eggs. Eggs are perhaps as much influenced by methods of cooking as by mere keeping, and I may remark in passing that the examples of the most violent egg-poisoning which I have known have occurred to individuals who, having manifested the idiosyncrasy to some extent at home, had incautiously partaken of articles containing eggs whilst travelling abroad. Amongst various other articles of diet respecting which peculiar susceptibilities are frequently shown, we have honey, tea, coffee, various fruits and vegetables, and various forms of alcoholic beverages. Cases of what deserve to be known as *tea-poisoning* are probably by no means infrequent, but the medical adviser who, having become cognizant of some of these, should straightway proceed to discourage the use of this beverage by all, would be making a very wide departure alike from the laws of clinical induction and common sense. We have to deal with idiosyncrasy, and must apply our knowledge under the limitations of its laws. It must be remembered, however, as I have already asserted, that idiosyncrasy by no means declines to enter into partnership with other causes of functional disturbance more easy to be understood. The varying state of the patient's health at different periods of life, and varying habits as regards diet at different times, may conceal or bring into unusual prominence an idiosyncrasy which is itself a permanent condition. In many patients susceptibility to the influence of tea is much increased by taking certain wines, notably champagne, and is diminished by malt liquors and the red wines. As a rough rule, all idiosyncrasies become aggravated when the tone of the system is low, and many of them pass into almost absolute abeyance under conditions of unusual vigor and health.

Idiosyncrasy in respect to tobacco displays itself in two forms, and one of them is of unusual interest, since it exemplifies a class of idiosyncrasies which are very apt to be misunderstood. I refer to those in which the individual susceptibility is not displayed immediately on the incidence of the exciting influence, but waits, it may be, for a long time, and until possibly other conditional causes come to its assistance. A little thought will probably supply most of us with examples of this class of idiosyncrasies, and they are very important in practice. A man who has drunk tea all his life, and largely, may rather suddenly find that it is almost poisonous to him, and may then recollect that one or more of his relations have never from childhood been able to take it. It is the same with eggs, fish, and certain kinds of wine, and so also with various drugs, and in all these instances it is, I believe, quite possible that the display of the idiosyncratic susceptibility may be only temporary. In some instances we may discover in some change in the mode of life or habits of diet, or in advancing age and possibly some visceral degeneration, an explanation of the newly-discovered peculiarity, but in other cases nothing can be found.

Tobacco, I think, stands curiously alone amongst the articles in human use in that it almost invariably in the first instance acts as a powerful poison, and that tolerance can be acquired quickly and certainly by almost every one. There are, however, great differences in the degree of susceptibility, and in the case with which habituation is obtained. Many never do obtain it, and although this in most cases may be merely the result of want of perseverance, there is a certain number in whom it would appear that the primary idiosyncrasy is insuperable. Many persons who have acquired tolerance of one kind of tobacco remain susceptible to others, and after having been habitual smokers for years, may be made very ill by inadvertently using an unaccustomed kind. Many smokers, I believe, recognize periods during which the pipe disagrees with them, and they are obliged for a time to abandon it, and very curious symptoms, such as absolute suspension of the sexual appetite, etc., are sometimes with confidence alleged as consequences of its excessive use. But the cases which are of most interest in connection with our present subject are those in which without any excess and in persons who have been for long thoroughly habituated, tobacco suddenly begins to act as a poison without causing any distaste or any conspicuous derangement. These patients are often quite unaware of what it is which is hurting them. They lose appetite and become nervous, and amongst the most conspicuous symptoms is a very marked failure of sight. This failure differs from all other forms of amaurotic amblyopia. It always affects simultaneously and equally both eyes; it begins very insidiously, and having no other symptom than diminution in acuity of vision, is often scarcely recognized by its subject until at the end of six weeks or two months he finds that he can only read the largest type. When at its height the optic disc is usually red and a little hazy, and at a later stage it becomes decidedly pale. If the patient will for a while leave off smoking he will regain his sight almost to a certainty, but, however perfect may be his apparent recovery, the disc is almost always left pale. He may resume the habit after awhile without much risk of relapse if he keeps to strict moderation, and in some cases recovery takes place, although the abstinence has never been complete.

Such are some of the principal facts respecting Tobacco Amaurosis. I have felt justified in stating them in this positive manner because I published in a series of reports some years ago in the 'Ophthalmic Journal' and the Royal Medical and Chirurgical Society's 'Transactions' very full details respecting them. That the symptoms in question are really due to tobacco I cannot feel the slightest doubt. I have seen no cases quite parallel to them either in women or in non-smoking men. If in these two classes of patients similar symptoms should be presented, which is very rare, I believe that they always progress without interruption to almost total blindness. Tobacco amaurosis rarely happens to novices in smoking, and seldom except to those who are liberal in the indulgence. Half an ounce of shag per day has been the usual allowance in the cases which I have collected. In support of my interpretation of the facts I may briefly advert to the history of our knowledge of them. Long before the ophthalmoscope-diagnosis was made out, Dr. Mackenzie, of Glasgow, and several French observers, had recognized the malady, and alluding to the difficulty met with in persuading its subjects to abandon the habit, Dr. Mackenzie had used the expression, "There are many who would rather smoke than see." Mr. Wordsworth, at Moorfields, was, I believe, one of the first who studied the opthalmoscope-diagnosis, and he held that the conditions displayed by the disc were pathognomonic. It was to his teaching that I was chiefly indebted for my first interest in the subject.

I must hasten to the narration of certain facts which show that this disease is really a matter of idiosyncrasy, and that we ought, by recognizing this fact, to explain the circumstance that such a very small proportion of smokers ever suffer from it. This immunity of the greater number and the picking out of one here and one there has been a great stumbling-block to many in the way of accepting this doctrine. I cannot think that it ought to have been so if due allowance be made for the influence of idiosyncrasy. The facts to which I first alluded as supporting the belief that this influence is really at work are the following:—Not very unfrequently the subject of tobacco amaurosis is one who was well aware of his susceptibility, who had experienced unusual difficulty in learning to smoke, and who had never been able to change with impunity from one kind of tobacco to another. Some years ago a young man came under my care who was a smoker, and who had smokers' amaurosis. Subsequently his mother, who did not smoke, came to me for an almost similar state of things, and I then learned that a nephew of hers, a smoker, had suffered just like his cousin, and had been under the care of my colleague, Mr. Hulke. I applied to Mr. Hulke for his diagnosis, and he kindly sent me a copy of his notes, showing that he had considered it a tobacco case. Here, then, we have three near relations presenting the same form of disease. In the woman, who did not smoke, the disease did not show itself until twenty years later in life than in the two young men who did, and in them, on abstinence, the disease was arrested, whilst in her, in whom no change of habit could be made, it increased. Can we doubt that we have here an instance of family proclivity?

I have yet to mention a stronger case in proof that special susceptibility may exist in a family. A hard-worked Welsh clergyman, had been accustomed to irregular meals and had consumed, in large quantities, a cheap, strong tobacco. He became nervous, and almost blind, and he recovered on giving up smoking. He told me subsequently that two of his brothers, farmers, had experienced precisely similar symptoms, and apparently in connection with the same cause. I did not see either of them, but I believe both were, like himself, almost wholly cured by abstinence from smoking. These two groups of cases, in each of which more than one member of the same family suffered from the same cause, bear to my mind very strong evidence in favor of the opinion that it is under the laws of idiosyncrasy that we must seek the explanation of chronic tobacco poisoning. It occurs to those in whom the nervous system, possibly the nervous tissue, has susceptibilities which are not shared alike by other members of the community. I have alluded to the fact that this susceptibility is not usually simple or immediate, as in the case of arsenic; it is almost always in those who have been long accustomed to smoking that these nerve phenomena occur, and they are probably indicative of a state approaching to saturation. If it be asked what are the other contributory causes which assist in producing the outbreak, I should be inclined to suggest that very varied influences which reduce tone may help; over-work and anxiety may assist, and so probably may the sudden loss of outdoor exercise. I do not think that the use of stimulants is often a contributory cause, at any rate, not unless to such extent as to interfere with appetite for food. Many facts which have come under my notice suggest that total abstainers from alcoholic beverages, if they smoke freely, in much more danger of chronic tobacco-poisoning than those who drink them.

Respecting idiosyncrasies as regards arsenic, I have to remark that they are not nearly so marked nor so common as those respecting some other drugs. I have met with exceedingly few cases in which small doses disagreed. It is very exceptional indeed that a patient complains of inconvenience at the outset of a course. Usually, symptoms occur after the drug has been to some extent pushed, and they for the most part necessitate its discontinuance or reduction. I am alluding now to the well-known symptoms of conjunctival irritation and pain in the stomach and bowels. Respecting these, I think, tolerance is never obtained, and if once they have occurred they are prone to occur again if the same doses are given. In English practice, individual susceptibility to arsenic does not seem to vary much. Most persons, as I have said, can take it, and very few can take more than a certain dose. I have never myself seen a case in which it could be pushed beyond a certain point without definite disagreement. The most remarkable fact in reference to idiosyncrasy is its occasional production of the form of neuritis which we know as herpes zoster. It is now more than ten years since I published a series of cases illustrating the occurrence of herpes zoster in patients who were taking arsenic, and since then I have

3

seen so many other examples of it that I cannot entertain the slightest doubt as to the direct connection between the two. The herpes eruption may occur in the forehead, face, or trunk, and it is wholly indistinguishable from the herpes in these regions which is not due to arsenic. It runs the usual course and disappears after its normal duration, whether the arsenic be continued or not. The patient does not, as a rule, show any constitutional symptoms of arsenic intolerance, and it is almost invariably the case that he has taken the drug for some weeks before the symptom appears. The advent may now and then be delayed until a week or ten days after the course has been suspended. A precisely similar interval is sometimes seen in cases of sympathetic ophthalmitis, in which affection—probably, also, a form of neuritis—the inflammation of the second eye may begin to develop a week or ten days after the entire removal, by excision, of its cause. These facts would suggest that the neuritis is in each instance slow in its stages, and that, having been once initiated, its local processes cannot be stopped. The number of those who show arsenical herpes is very small in proportion to those who escape, and, if it is to occur at all, I think it always happens during a first course. I have never seen it in a patient who had been accustomed to the drug for a long time. Thus, its occurrence must certainly rank as the result of an idiosyncrasy; and this suggestion opens the way for the further one—that we ought, perhaps, always to regard herpes zoster as, in the main, an indication of personal peculiarity. It certainly does not appear that all persons are equally liable to it, since it happens to but very few, and is never associated with any special form of ill-health. Excepting the single fact, just alluded to, of its occasional production by arsenic, we know of no causes which can evoke it. I have seen arsenic produce herpes in two different regions at the same time, but I do not remember to have ever witnessed a second attack in the same individual. In reference to this, however, it is but fair to add that I have usually carefully avoided this drug after an attack of shingles, since the latter is often a very serious trouble. A few persons—a very few—are liable to the occurrence of an eruption of herpetic vesicles over and over again in the same part of the skin, and, as is well known, examples of recurring herpes on mucous membrane are common, as, for instance, on the lips and genitals. Sometimes recurrences take place once a month, or even oftener, the eruptions always passing through the usual stages, and undergoing a speedy and spontaneous cure. There is never any peculiarity of health to be made out in explanation of these cases, and they must, I suppose, rank as idiosyncrasies. Homœopathists are welcome to make what use they can of the fact that arsenic will often cure these cases and prevent the recurrence. I have repeatedly seen herpes of this kind remain in abeyance for many months whilst the patient was taking arsenic, and show itself again when the drug was suspended. I have seen one case which to some extent offers an exception to some of the statements which I have just made, inasmuch as the patient was liable repeatedly to an eruption from arsenic. The eruption always came soon after beginning the remedy, and he was well accustomed to its use. The patient is a gentleman now near to sixty, who has suffered from psoriasis most of his life, and for whom in early life Sir Benjamin Brodie prescribed arsenic. He has often taken it since, and its usual effect is as stated. On one occasion he took it in order to show me the character of the eruption produced. It had been called "eczema," and, although it certainly had the local features of an erythematous eczema, yet it occurred, like herpes, unsymmetrically on one arm in large patches, which disappeared spontaneously after a few days.

LECTURE III.

Mr. President and Gentlemen,—I hope I have made it sufficiently clear that I am not purposing to trouble you with any list of idiosyncrasies. As well for your relief as my own exculpation, it is perhaps desirable that I should again make this statement. What I said about egg-poisoning in my last lecture was intended to suffice as an illustration of what is possible, indeed, I would suggest not infrequent, in reference to a whole group of food-idiosyncrasies. The same remark applies to the somewhat detailed discussion on the susceptibilities in reference to tobacco. We are engaged in the examination of the laws of idiosyncrasy, and not in any attempt to record exhaustively its facts. I shall bring before you no more narratives of cases or statements as to facts than may seem absolutely necessary to illustrate the general laws to which we refer. In Monday's lecture we glanced briefly at certain peculiarities of structure which are sometimes met with in external parts which are both congenital and hereditary. For these I proposed the name of structural idiosyncrasies, and asked that we should apply the knowledge that we can easily gain respecting them to those which are much more obscure, from the fact that they are betrayed only by derangement of function.

I next alluded to certain forms of inflammatory disease not present at birth, and in most cases not commencing until a considerable period after it, but concerning which the general facts suggest that they must be due to some inborn peculiarity of the structure implicated. Lastly, I adverted to examples of complicated or secondary idiosyncrasy in which the individual peculiarity is not displayed immediately on the application of its exciting cause, but waits, as it were, for the co-operation of other influences. We found one of our best illustrations of this in the chronic poisoning, denoted chiefly by amblyopia, to which smokers are in exceptionable instances liable. I concluded my lecture by a brief allusion to idiosyncrasies in reference to arsenic, and was obliged by

36

want of time to defer till to-day what I have to bring before you on the important subject of the iodides and similar salts. I shall be compelled to omit altogether what I had prepared in reference to belladonna, opium, and certain other drugs, an omission which I shall regret the less because, as just said, I am seeking only for illustrations of law and of these perhaps we shall have enough.

The iodides and bromides offer us, indeed, such excellent and various illustrations of the laws of idiosyncrasy that I am almost tempted to wish that I had excluded all others, and thus secured more time for the consideration of them. The modes in which these salts can produce disagreement are exceedingly varied, and concern very different parts of the system, whilst many of them are displayed by the skin in a manner which permits of their easy identification and examination. Not even the syphilitic virus itself is capable of producing a greater multiplicity of pathological changes in the integument. Now it is a hæmorrhage, now a thrombosis, now an erythema, now a bulla; the commonest of all forms is an acne, but in addition to it and those which I have named we may have at the same time pustules, button-like tubercles, and in aggravated cases enormous soft tuberous growths.

If time had permitted me I should have taken occasion to advert also to a topic of much importance to us in operative practice, and should have suggested that in a considerable number of the accidents with anæsthetics it is idiosyncrasy which we encounter. Many of the deaths from chloroform occur to persons apparently in perfect health, and when only small quantities have been given and with every possible precaution. Such cases ought probably to be placed side by side with those in which individual susceptibility becomes unexpectedly revealed to us in reference to such drugs as opium, belladonna, and the like. We waste our labor when we search for proof of heart disease, or some flaw in the apparatus, or some want of care in the administration. The last patient in whom, under my own care, we came near to a fatal event with chloroform, was a man at Moorfields, in whose case extraction of cataract was about to be performed. He would certainly have died but for the vigorous use of artificial respiration and the nitrite of amyl. In discussing the case afterwards I was reminded by our house-surgeon that three years before, when the other eye was operated on, the same man had caused us alarm by precisely similar symptoms. The occurrence had unfortunately been forgotten. It is probable that there are persons in whom, owing to peculiarity of nerve organization, and not in the least to anything which we can recognize as ill health, the inhalation of chloroform will always cause an extreme depression of the heart's action. In such, if the precaution of giving beforehand a dose of opium, alcohol, or ether, be omitted, there is the utmost risk of a fatal event. Probably each anæsthetic has its related conditions of idiosyncrasy.

I have passed over also another subject, owing to want of time, which has considerable surgical interest. It is the influence of inherited structural peculiarities in favoring the occurrence of lesions which at first sight suggest no suspicion of such origin. Examples we have of this in the easy occurrence of dislocation, owing to peculiarity in joint formation; and the proneness to intussusception of the bowels, owing to the cæcum and ascending colon being provided with a mesentery. I have several times known the tendency to intussusception show itself in several members of the same family, and in one of the most marked instances in which several of the children had died of it in succession the condition referred to was found at the autopsy of one of them.

I now turn to the subject of the idiosyncrasies in reference to the iodides and bromides. It seems probable that the difference in form which the inflammation of the skin assumes is dependent upon the peculiarities of the individual, for if the patient has shown a tendency to an unusual development of the iodide rash on one occasion, and the same salt be given to him on another, even after a long interval of time, it will produce exactly the same effect. This I have witnessed repeatedly. Idiosyncrasies as regards the iodide are not manifested solely by the skin, are perhaps not primary in it, and are seldom confined to it. Congestions, with excessive secretion, of certain tracts of mucous membrane, are of yet more frequent occurrence than are skin rashes, but they differ from the latter in that they are, in a majority of instances, only transitory. An eruption on the skin, once developed by the iodide, persists—and indeed becomes increased—so long as the drug is given; sometimes, even after it has been suspended. The iodide coryza, as it is called, on the contrary, seldom lasts more than a few days; or if it becomes chronic, always subsides into a slight affair. Thus the one would appear to imply idiosyncrasy in a far less degree than the other, and this suspicion is borne out by the observation that in those who suffer from any of the more serious forms of skin eruptions, there are usually other evidences that the drug is producing injurious effects. The tone of the nervous system is always lowered by it, and sometimes to an alarming extent. There is, perhaps, no drug that can be mentioned respecting which idiosyncrasy is so common and variations in its degree so great. I have repeatedly seen doses of only half a grain produce, in the course of a couple of days, definite symptoms of poisoning; and, on the other hand, I have known a patient swallow an ounce and a half a day of the best Apothecaries' Hall iodide for a week together without any special effect, except a feeling of lassitude and want of tone. It is also very remarkable how, in a large majority of cases in which definite and peculiar susceptibility is at first manifested, tolerance may subsequently be attained, and doses of ten, twenty, thirty times the amount given without obvious effect. Probably there is no drug respecting which the assertion can be more easily demonstrated, that it is not the dose, but its effect, which we should regard. It by no means follows that because a patient has an idiosyncrasy against some drug or article of diet, that we ought wholly to abstain from its use. Rather this susceptibility, in the majority of cases, proves that in him minute doses will effect the cure first as efficiently as larger ones in others. I have repeatedly cured tertiary ulcerations of the throat and skin in patients in whom I was assured iodide was a poison in all doses, by giving it in quantities of half, or even a third, of a grain. In the year 1862, M. Bazin, of Paris, an excellent specialist, and at the same time an excellent physician, described a new disease under the name of *Hydroa*. Of this malady he recognized several varieties, one like varicella, one resembling smallpox. On reading M. Bazin's descriptions I was at once struck by the closeness with which they applied to several cases which had been under my own care, and in 1870 I wrote in the ' British Medical Journal' a report on " hydroa," quoting M. Bazin's descriptions, and recording my own cases together with others supplied to me by my friends. I had previously been to Paris and seen M. Bazin's models. At that time neither of us had any idea of the usual cause of the eruption, nor, I believe, had any of our readers or critics. One of the latter suggested that we had not named it correctly, and that it was only an " urticaria bullosa," but in doing this he gave us no clue to its cause. At this date we all knew of the acne which so commonly results from the iodide, but were not aware that this salt could in connection with idiosyncrasy produce other symptoms so much more formidable. In the session of 1869, Dr. Cholmeley brought before the Clinical Society an example of a remarkable confluent eruption produced by the bromide; several papers had also appeared in Paris on the subject, and subsequently I convinced myself that almost all the examples of the disease to which we had given a new name were really the bullous form of the iodide eruption. From that time to this I have seen but very few examples of "hydroa" except as the consequence of iodides or bromides. It will be seen that we had made no error in observation, but had simply described and named a disease which was new to us, and new to medical literature, but of which at the time we had not discovered the cause. When the cause was found the name became of little importance. As already hinted, however, we have by no means in mentioning the iodide acne, the iodide "hydroa," concluded the list of symptoms due to this drug. Respecting a case which I have to mention in the next group, I shall not be surprised if many remain still in doubt as to whether it ought to be placed in this position. A man came to me at the London Hospital covered with large soft tumors, some of them as big as a child's fist. They occurred chiefly on his face, chest, and limbs. That I may avoid a lengthy description, I will simply refer you to the sketch which hangs on the wall, which is a rough copy from an excellent drawing which I now display. It will be enough to say that the moment I saw it I believed it to be an iodide eruption, and that my diagnosis was based upon the recollection of other cases, unquestionably due to that cause, which I had previously seen. The man had just been discharged from another hospital, and on inquiry I found that during his month's stay in it he had been steadily taking the iodide in increasing doses the whole time. The eruption was not present in the least before the drug was begun. The patient died, within a fortnight of his admission under my care, from exhaustion, apparently due to the extent of surface implicated. The post mortem revealed nothing which threw further light upon the cause of his malady. It seemed probable that he had never had syphilis. He had gone into the hospital on account of another complaint, and when the eruption appeared it was considered to be syphilitic, and instead of suspending the remedy, its dose was increased. The dose was, however, never more than fifteen grains three times a day. To those who are still inclined to doubt whether this terrible eruption was really due to the iodide—and I admit I have no right to be surprised if the number comprises all my audience —I would put the question, What else could it be? The microscope showed in the tubers only the results of common inflammation, and there was nothing in the least suggestive of malignancy. Above all, I would ask that a careful comparison be made with the other drawings from another case which I have placed by its side. It will be seen that the two closely resemble each other, and differ only in the greater sever- ity of the one I have just described. In all essential features of the eruption they are exactly alike. Now there is not room for the slightest doubt as to the cause of the eruption in the second case. It was pro- duced by the bromide of potassium, and it occurred in connection with that drug twice to the same child. I may here remark that I know of no difference between the eruption due to iodides and those due to bromides. The same variety occurs, I think, in both, and the general laws as to idiosyncrasy are the same. The iodide, however, depresses the system far more than the bromide. The eruptions produced by bromides are, I think, attended by less constitutional disturbance, even when locally very severe, than are those due to iodides. A case well illustrating this came under my notice a few weeks ago. I was asked by a medical friend to see an infant in whose case the diagnosis had first been varicella, and next smallpox. Complete isolation had been en- forced, but as the eruption had steadily got worse, and the child now at the end of a month remained perfectly well as to health, all had become convinced that there was a mistake. I have mentioned the names which had been given to the eruption as the best means of suggesting the appearances it at first assumed, and I may add that the surgeon who attended the case was an experienced and sagacious man. The infant, when I saw it, was fat and smiling, but with its face and all four ex- tremities absolutely covered with large buttons of most formidable ap- pearance. Many of them had scabs, but none of them had ulcerated much. At first I was told that the eruption was present before a medical man was consulted, and before any medicine had been given, but on pressing for accurate dates, I found that my suspicion was correct, and that the surgeon was first consulted for a slight feverish cold, for which he prescribed small doses of bromide of potassium, and that the rash did not begin to appear till three days later. No suspicion having been entertained, the bromide had been continued until the day of my visit. My friend told me that he was very fond of the bromide for children, and had given it in thousands of cases, but had never before seen any eruption produced. In looking back on the experience of former years, I recollect several cases under my own care, and that of other surgeons, in whom I think there is great reason to suspect that persistence in the iodide caused death. They were cases in which an eruption which was probably due to it alone was mistaken for a specific one, and the drug pushed still further. In the report which I published in the Clinical Society's 'Transactions' I have published two cases in which our eyes were opened only just in time. They were all cases in which the salt had been continued for some weeks. It may be possible, however, for fatal poisoning to occur in connection with the first few doses. In the case of a man admitted into the London Hospital some years ago, only two or three doses had been taken, and an eruption which looked like hæmorrhagic variola had been produced, together with such an amount of swelling about the neck and throat that nothing but the prompt performance of tracheotomy could have averted immediate death. The facts respecting this case were published by my colleague Dr. Stephen Mackenzie, and the same indefatigable observer has also placed upon record the most extraordinary example of iodide poisoning with which I am acquainted. In this instance, an infant, aged five months, died of iodic purpura after a single dose of only two grains and a half.

The domain of idiosyncrasy in respect to Specific Fevers is exceedingly important as regards both the physician and the surgeon, and I shall make no attempt to distinguish arbitrarily between their interest in this matter. That which the surgeon is familiar with in the case of syphilis and those remote and exceptional sequelæ of measles, scarlatina, and smallpox which come under his care, may be used to throw light upon the facts which fall under the observation of the physician in the

earlier stages of these latter maladies.   There is probably no good reason
for believing that the specific animal poisons can vary in their intensity
beyond certain narrow limits.   Different epidemics of scarlet fever and
small-pox do unquestionably vary somewhat, but after all, the limits of
deviation from average intensity observed in different epidemics are as
nothing compared with what we witness in different individuals attacked
in the same epidemic and apparently under like circumstances.   In the
latter case we see constantly that it is possible for two individuals infected from the same source and with the same virus to show the one
an eruption consisting only of a few spots almost unattended by fever,
whilst the other develops a confluent or even hæmorrhagic exanthem,
which will prove fatal in a few days.   Is it possible to give any explanation of these individual differences, except by attributing them to individual peculiarities, and when these peculiarities arise to an extreme
height, can we name them more conveniently than as idiosyncrasies?
I will endeavor to illustrate the subject by facts which have come under
my own personal cognizance.   The portraits which I produce exhibit a
gangrenous and ulcerative eruption which occurs in connection with
varicella.   They are, in fact, a peculiar form of varicella in which the
eruption tends to persist and the individual vesicles ulcerate or become
gangrenous.   The evidence upon which I venture this unqualified
assertion is, I think, conclusive, for this eruption has been observed
repeatedly with the history that in the first instance it was supposed to
be chicken-pox, and whilst chicken-pox was in the family; and in a few
yet more definite cases, the surgeon who identified the gangrenous case
was the witness at the same time of varicella in its ordinary mild form
in the patient's brothers and sisters.   The facts have fallen under the
observation not of myself alone, but of many others, and they receive
important incidental corroboration from several narratives published
long ago, and without full perception of the interpretation of the facts.
My present object is to cite them simply in proof of the possible influence of idiosyncrasy in modifying the course of an exanthem.   The
case to which the portrait which I next show belongs, was that of an
infant to all appearance in perfect health, who had several brothers and
sisters, all healthy, who had all been vaccinated at the usual time with
the usual results.   In this child, however, vaccination was followed on

the seventh day by a general eruption on the skin; which on the tenth day looked like ordinary small-pox, which subsequently became gangrenous, and caused death at the end of a fortnight. The state of the child's skin at the time of its death is well shown in the portraits.[1] It will be seen to be covered by spots and patches of gangrene, the sphacelus involving the whole thickness of the skin. There is no form of variola known which in the least resembles this condition, and none will suggest, I think, that diagnosis. On the other hand, there is a well-known eruption, usually slight and mild but occasionally very definite, which occurs after vaccination, to which the term vaccinia exanthem is appropriate. My suggestion is that this eruption bears the same relation to the ordinary mild vaccinia rash which gangrenous varicella does to the common type of chicken-pox, and that its exceptional severity was due to individual idiosyncrasy.

I show next another portrait from a similar case which was observed by Mr. William Stokes in Dublin, to whose kindness I am indebted for the portrait. The general facts were similar to those in my own case, with the difference that the eruption occurred a day or two earlier after vaccination, that the patches of gangrene were more irregular and more superficial, and that the child survived. I do not know that any other examples of gangrenous vaccinia have as yet been published, but I have no doubt that such will in the future be observed. I have now related some extreme instances illustrating the influence of idiosyncrasy in causing severity of exanthems which are usually very mild. Probably there are quite as striking examples of the converse, instances in which the specific animal poisons pass through the system and produce little or no obvious effect. It may be that these are much more common, and that they go far to explain some of the great apparent irregularities in the course of the exanthemata. We often meet with individuals who tell us, for instance, that they have never had scarlet fever or measles, although they were exposed in childhood at the same time that their brothers and sisters suffered; and we often see these diseases go through a family and leave one or more children apparently untouched. Still oftener will it happen that one or several individuals under such cir-

---

[1] One of these is copied to illustrate my paper on this subject in this year's volume of the "Medico-Chirurgical Transactions."

cumstances will show only a very slight febrile ailment, without any of the more characteristic symptoms of the disease, whilst others suffer severely.

It has happened to me recently to witness a family epidemic of scarlatina which remarkably illustrates what I wish to say. In mentioning its details, let it not be supposed that I think that it illustrates anything unusual; on the contrary, I believe that similar occurrences fall very frequently within the experience of those engaged in general practice.

My facts are briefly these: a child was affected with sore-throat and feverishness, but had no rash whatever, and beyond a slight fur, no change in the condition of the tongue. She was well in a day or two, and nothing subsequently occurred to her. Four days later another child sickened with exactly similar symptoms, but more marked, and in her the usual rash of scarlatina soon appeared; and subsequently a little boy went through the same course of events. Both of these observed precisely the same periods as regards the progress of the disease; both had nose-bleeding on the same day, followed by rheumatism beginning in the same joints, the wrists, and both had great swelling of the cervical lymphatic glands. Subsequently an older sister, who was believed to have had it some years ago, went through a rather sharp attack. Thus, I take it, there can be no doubt that the disease in this instance was scarlet fever; but to prevent any question on the score of diagnosis I may add that one of the patients was seen by Dr. Gee.

It is to what I have next to state that the chief interest attaches. The child who was the first ill, and who had but a day's sore-throat, no tongue affection, no rash, no peeling, was subsequently most fully exposed to the risk of infection, and did not take it, conclusively proving, I think, that the trivial illness she experienced was the fully developed malady so far as her idiosyncrasy permitted it to show itself. But I have other facts yet more curious. Almost the whole family, and it was a large one, suffered one after the other, during the two or three weeks that the disease was in the house, from sore-throats and a day or two of feverishness. Several of them had never had scarlet fever before, but as to some others, it was doubtful. In all, the cervical lymphatics swelled more or less, but in no instance was there the slightest peeling or any sort of sequela. I have yet to add that, when the first child had sore-throat, I was at once told that the family of a cottager living at a short distance from the house had just been suffering from similar throats. This cottager was the milkman, and there had also been personal communication between the two houses. On inquiring at this cottage, I found that the father, mother, and two grown-up daughters had all in succession had sore throats, attended for a day or two with rather sharp febrile illness, but in no single instance had any rash been observed, nor had any peeling of the skin followed. They were not known to have had scarlet fever on any former occasion, and laughed at the suggestion that what they had now had was it. It may be that after all it was not, but the dates fitted well with the possibility that the first of the children affected had got the contagion from this source. The inference which I wish to draw from such narratives as this is, that it is possible for the individual peculiarity of patients—a peculiarity which may be hereditary and may affect many individuals in the same family—to so far modify and minify the course of an exanthematic fever as to make its recognition quite impossible, and that we ought to seek for the explanation of these remarkable differences, amounting in many instances to almost total suppression, not in variableness in the degree of epidemic virulence, nor in the hygienic surroundings, nor in anything which can properly be called the state of health of the patient, but in that of which we can give no other explanation than that it must rank as an idiosyncrasy.

It is needless to point out what a pitfall of fallacy is here opened for the feet of the investigator. How easily may we find ourselves attributing to influences which were wholly inoperative, results which must simply be put aside as those which we ought to have expected under the known laws of idiosyncrasy. I will leave for the present the examination of those laws as they influence the course of a certain other specific fever. This is the time at which I ought properly to mention the facts which, in the case of the protracted fever known as syphilis, illustrate its extreme inequality of incidence in different persons. I must not, however, enter into any details now, and I leave them aside the more willingly because the facts to which I refer are matters of universal knowledge. We all know how differently chancres behave in different persons; how they may become phagedænic or sloughing without our being able to assign any cause for the peculiarity. We know, also, that the syphilitic rash in many cases is wholly omitted, together with the rest of the train of secondary phenomena. We know also how, when secondary symptoms do appear, how infinitely variable they may be in form and in severity. A roseola, a lichen, a psoriasis, a rupia, an eruption indistinguishable from variola—such are a few of the forms which we frequently see. Impressed by these startling differences, good observers have tried to make out that there are different kinds of virus, but all the facts are in opposition to such hypotheses. I must content myself by suggesting that they are due to inherent differences in the individuals who receive the virus, and must now pass on to other topics.

Let me next remark that, not only is the sphere of individual peculiarity almost unbounded in its power of modifying the force of the primary outbreak of an exanthem, but that it exercises a great influence in determining who shall and who shall not, suffer from complications and sequelæ. Under this latter term I am alluding rather to what may be called accidental sequelæ; the inflammations of various organs and parts which occur exceptionally and at some little distance of time, and which often bring the patient under the care of the surgeon. The peeling of the skin, and possibly also the nephritic desquamation which follows scarlatina, are sometimes classed as sequelæ, but are really parts of the primary disease. As I think my narrative has conclusively shown, peeling of the skin is not a sequel of scarlet fever *per se,* but of one of the symptoms of scarlet fever, namely, of *dermatitis;* to which it is always proportional, and of which it is the necessary consequence. Inflammations of the ears, and of the bones or joints, stand, however, in a different category, and so does the ophthalmia tarsi, which often follows measles, and the pruriginous affections of the skin which are not infrequent after both vaccinia and varicella. When these events happen, they occur probably not by any means as necessary parts of the disease, but rather as revealing idiosyncrasy in the individual. Inflammations of the ear and allied affections may possibly in some instances reveal diathesis rather than idiosyncrasy. That is, it may be that they occur because the patient is distinctly scrofulous, or the subject of some other form of recognized ill-health. Even as regards them, however, I much doubt whether this is always true, and respecting the affections of the skin to which I have referred, I am sure that they often occur to those who are in good health, and that they are proof of idiosyncrasy only.

Differences in the degree of irritability of the skin are common, and may proceed to great length. Flea-bites, woollen clothing, nettle-stings, and the like, produce on different persons extremely different results. Urticaria is a form of dermatitis of which probably but few persons are susceptible, and in those in whom it occurs it demonstrates or reveals this susceptibility and nothing more. The patient who gets nettle-rash whenever he eats lobster may yet be able to digest lobster with as little inconvenience as other people. It is his skin, or perhaps the nerves of his skin, in which the susceptibility alone lies. In this suggestion rests, so far as I can see, the real explanation of the maladies which have been grouped together under the name of *Prurigo*. There is no one disease to which that name is applicable. What we witness is the power of various causes of local irritation to provoke pruriginous dermatitis in those in whom idiosyncratic susceptibility exists. Now it is the presence of pediculi which is the starting-point; in other cases of fleas; in yet others the occurrence of an exanthem, such as varicella; whilst in all, the morbid condition, once initiated, is kept up by the patient's unwise efforts to relieve it, and by the mere fact of its having got possession. I repeat, there is no such disease as "Prurigo," a malady which has been described by a high authority as if it were self-existent, and alike causeless and cureless; but there are plenty of persons born with that peculiar irritability of skin in which a variety of causes may evoke the symptoms to which that name has been given.

We may probably, with much confidence, place diphtheria and erysipelas side by side as diseases,—or rather type forms of the inflammatory process,—which obey parallel laws. Probably no human being is exempt from the liability to them, but at the same time it seems certain that the degree of proneness varies very much in different individuals, is persistent through life, prevails in families, and is matter of inheritance. Thus, then, we assert for both the existence not unfrequently of a sort of constitutional predisposition to which the term diathesis, or even in some instances, that of idiosyncrasy, is applicable. Both may become contagious, and of both exposure to direct contagion is probably by far the most efficient mode of production. Many persons will take them by contagion in whom other causes would have proved abortive. But both are capable of spontaneous origin or, to speak more correctly, may be produced by exposure to certain non-specific influences, such as the ordinary causes of catarrh, injuries, sewer gas, and some others. It is most important that all who value accurate classification should deny both as regards erysipelas and diphtheria their right to rank with those fevers which are due to specific animal poisons. With these, as it seems to me, neither of them has any real affinities. In both, I repeat, that with which we have to deal is a personal and inherited peculiarity, giv-ing proclivity when certain exciting causes are brought to bear, to pecu-liar forms of inflammatory action. In both the disease is probably local at its origin; in both it spreads locally by the contagion of con-tinuity of tissue, and in both constitutional symptoms result which are in some ratio with the extent and severity of the local action. Neither of them in the least protects the individual from future attacks; indeed, and although in each single attacks are common enough, yet it is gen-erally acknowledged that those who have suffered once are more prone than others to suffer again, and in both there are not infrequent in-stances of proclivity lasting through many years.

In erysipelas the essential feature is a spreading inflammation of lym-phatic spaces in the skin producing great œdema, and usually great en-largement of blood-vessels. In diphtheria we have a spreading inflam-mation of a mucous membrane, attended by œdema, dilatation of blood-vessels, and the formation, in greater or less quantity, of a fibrin-ous pellicle. Although I mention skin as the seat of the one and mucous membrane of the other, let it be distinctly understood that these are only the most usual sites; both may attack cellular tissue or wounds, and each may occasionally affect the usual territory of the other.

There may be some doubt as to how, when these inflammations affect repeatedly the same individual, the fact should be explained. It may be that one attack leaves a really increased proclivity to a second, or it may be that the first simply revealed a proclivity which had existed all

4

along, and of which the later ones are merely the manifestations without addition. Probably both explanations are true.

It is, I presume, not necessary that I should produce before this audience any citation of evidence in proof that a personal liability to erysipelas and diphtheria may be witnessed. All are familiar with them. It is probable that there are some slightly marked affinities with the diseases just named and such maladies as carbuncle, boils, and acne. Respecting all these we have the same questions to ask, how far are they dependent upon constitutional causes? and, how far upon those which are local? We may take it as certain that in all there is a double causation, and our task is to assign in each instance the relative share of each. In the first place we may say that the liability to acne, to boils, to carbuncles, is often a family matter, and is seen to occur with unusual frequency in relatives. It is often also a personal matter, as is proved by its persistence or recurrence at various periods of life. Further, the association of these maladies with more or less temporary disturbances of health, with diabetic dyspepsia, with constipation and defective tone, is a matter of constant observation.

Whoever has reflected, however, as to the real nature of carbuncular inflammation, will, I think, see reason to believe that its peculiarities are to a large extent local ones. Respecting both boils and carbuncles, it is the fact that the most efficient measures of treatment are those which appeal to the local condition. This is true of all the different measures in repute, however dissimilar at first sight they may appear. Some have for their object the protection of the inflamed area from further irritation, as when we cover up a boil or commencing carbuncle with leather plaster, others the subdual of the inflammation by means of cold and the like, as when we use an ice-bladder or a strong spirit lotion. Nor do those who adopt a time-honored practice of an early free incision depart from this principle, for their object is still the mitigation of local inflammation by the relief of tension, and by permitting the escape of contaminating matters. From acne, impetigo, and ecthyma to boils is in many cases a matter of degree, and that there is little or no real distinction between a large boil and a small carbuncle, all will, I think, admit. The age of the patient, and his special diathetic condition at the time, their site, the influence of different modes of local treatment, are the conditions which determine the final result.   If a boil occur in an elderly person, on the nape of the neck, where it is likely to be irritated by the shirt-collar, and especially if, instead of being systematically protected from the first, it be further bullied by premature squeezing and the like, it is very likely to pass on into a carbuncle.   I claim the strong testimony which has been borne by Sir James Paget and others to the efficiency of simply protective measures in preventing the development of small carbuncles, and obviating the supposed necessity for incision, as proof that local spreading is, in the main, due to local causes, and has no necessary connection with the general health.   In other words, it is not a thing which is inevitable.   On the other hand, we know of no internal remedy which possesses any marked power in arresting carbuncular inflammation

If now we ask, In what does the peculiarity of carbuncular inflammation consist? in what does a carbuncle differ from a boil?   I should be inclined to reply that it is solely in this tendency to spread.   The spreading is effected by contagion of continuity, and it has certain marked resemblances to what we observe in erysipelas.   A carbuncle might almost be defined to be *an erysipelatous boil* with the proviso that the expression is not intended to imply identity of inflammatory type, but only close similarity.   Throughout its whole course, and however extensive it may be, a carbuncle, in combination with its erysipelatous method of spreading, contains the characteristics of the furuncular process.   Its secretions and its core, or slough, are exactly like those of a boil, excepting that they are much more abundant.   In a general way there appears to be a natural tendency, independently of treatment, to the arrest of the process, and this is not generally observed in erysipelas.   In other words, erysipelatous inflammation is more intensely infective than is carbuncular.   I must, however, qualify even this admission of difference by reminding you, that carbuncular inflammation has such an injurious influence on health, that in all cases in which its spread continues in spite of treatment the patient quickly dies.   Thus many cases occur in which no proof is given of tendency to arrest.   It may easily be the fact that in some states of system, and some types of carbuncle, there is as little tendency to arrest as there is in phlegmonous erysipelas.

I fear I have wandered rather far from the subject of diathesis, but my argument, if I have succeeded in making it clear, is this; that there exists a certain state of tissue and constitution, different in each instance, which gives proclivity to diphtheria, to erysipelas, to acne, to boils, and to carbuncle, and that while the importance, the almost paramount importance in many instances, of local influences in exciting and aggravating is kept in mind, the diathesis in the background must not be forgotten. Further I have argued that carbuncle is the result of a sort of combination of the erysipelatous and furuncular types of inflammation. I feel sure that these views as to pathology will be found to fit well with therapeutics.

Tetanus is a malady so rare, that if we admit its possible spontaneous production without regard to previously existing proclivity, we must not expect to find many instances in proof that the latter does sometimes exist. Yet there are such, and possibly if looked for more than we might suppose. The influence of race is proved by the great liability both of infants and adults amongst the negroes, and also of certain animals. I have met with a few cases in English practice which appeared to imply that there might be an inherited proclivity to tetanus. A man who looked quite well walked into my room as an out patient at the Metropolitan Free Hospital and gave me his own diagnosis by declaring " I am going to have lockjaw." I found that he had recently had a slight wound on one hand, and that he was beginning to feel some stiffness of his jaws. His symptoms, however, were exceedingly slight, and his anxiety was caused by the fact that his father had died of tetanus. The poor fellow's foreboding was rapidly realized, and he died within a week.

Here, for the present, Mr. President, I must take leave of the subject of idiosyncrasy. I have endeavored to claim for these forms of individual peculiarity a much wider sphere of influence than is usually accorded to them. It is necessary, I am well aware, that one should exercise some scepticism in accepting doctrines of the kind which I have brought before you. To fall back on the suggestion of an idiosyncrasy is so easy that it may easily become the resort of intellectual sloth. We must not, however, be deterred by this consideration from the acceptance of such doctrines if they are true. That they are so within certain limits I cannot doubt, and the problem before us is to find those limits. If we fail to recognize, or if we forget, the influences of idiosyncrasy, we shall not only waste much time in our processes of clinical research, but we shall be in constant danger of coming to wrong conclusions by declining to accept evidence as to cause which is really sound, and of adopting false principles in reference to treatment.   In every example of a curious and unexpected form of disease, our minds should, I think, first ask the question, "How much of this may possibly be due to the individual peculiarities of its subject?"   We are often on a wrong track if we seek to make external influences explain the whole.

Let me add, in conclusion, and it seems to me of great practical moment, that the individual peculiarities of all patients should be carefully studied, and that they should themselves be made intelligently acquainted with them.   There are few of us without our idiosyncrasies, and their variety is innumerable.   If it should become the custom for parents to record some sort of life-history of their children in permanent form from the birth or infancy onwards, noting all the peculiarities in an individual by the aid of medical observation, not only would much be done in the way of preventing subsequent errors in the treatment of disease, but valuable contributions would be made to our knowledge of its real nature.   It is not only as regards the prescription of our drugs that a knowledge of our patient's peculiarities becomes important to use in practice.   The advice we have to give in respect to places of residence, mode of life, and of general management are often of far more importance than the medicine prescribed.   Its wisdom or the reverse may depend on our knowledge or ignorance of the individual peculiarities, and those peculiarities frequently do not display themselves in any of the existing symptoms, but can be recognized and revealed only by a correctly kept life-history.

LECTURE IV.

Mr. President and Gentlemen,—We turn to-day to a new department of our subject. I have been dealing hitherto with fixed inborn peculiarities which are for the most part beyond our explanation, but in consequence of which disease in individuals may assume very peculiar features. How peculiar and exceptional those features may be I have illustrated by the production of cases of bullous, pruriginous, and even gangrenous varicella, and of two examples of gangrenous vaccinia. I have also reminded you of the great differences in different individuals in the type and severity of syphilis, and I have shown, too, how, not only may the exanthemata sometimes attain most unusual severity, but that not unfrequently all their usual symptoms may seem to be suppressed and the patient may pass through a complete attack scarcely knowing that he has been ill. We have further glanced at the facts which prove that the iodides and bromides, remedies in daily and most frequent use, and for the most part very harmless, may occasionally act as violent poisons. Lastly, I have urged that in many other morbid processes originating in connection with ordinary and known causes, or it may be from local infection, the peculiar constitution of the individual takes an important share as well in increasing the proclivity as in modifying the result. Instances of this I found in such diseases as diphtheria, erysipelas, and carbuncle. Respecting these and the other examples of personal proclivity or immunity which I have ventured to cite, I have maintained the same argument, that they are all independent of everything that is to be recognized in the state of health of the patient, and that they imply that which is conveniently known as idiosyncrasy. Much, indeed almost all, that I have advanced is, I am well aware, by no means novel. I have been dealing with old names and well-established doctrines, and my reason for bringing them before you has been, not so much the hope of being able to contribute new facts or theories of my own, as the desire to set in better order

54

that floating knowledge which is a general possession. In the lectures which are yet to come I shall restrict myself to the same design. I am going to ask your attention to a great number of topics, to many of which I shall advert with such brevity that it would not be possible for me to enforce original views even if I possessed them. The bond of connection which will associate these various subjects will be the endeavor to discover whether there exist any large groups of states of personal peculiarity giving special proclivity to diseases which can be suitably defined and named. If the reply to this question be in the affirmative—if we see reason for believing that those who become our patients do really differ one from another in respect to definite tendencies, which are of prolonged duration and upon the knowledge of which we can conveniently base not only our prognosis but our treatment, it will next be our duty to examine as to the real nature of those states and the laws under which they came into being and continue to exist. I have dismissed the consideration of temperaments as being when correctly limited an unproductive field of research, but in doing this I expressed a belief that the investigation of the diatheses stood in a very different position. In the one we deal with the peculiarities of race and the results of what may be termed breeding, in the latter we begin much nearer home and investigate the consequences of a variety of influences which are capable either separately or together of producing chronic disease. For, in fact, what we mean by a diathesis is little other than an exceedingly chronic disease. It is a disease or taint which lasts a lifetime, which may be active at times, and latent at times, and which may be handed on to another generation. If we accept as a definition of diathesis that it is *any condition of prolonged peculiarity of health giving proclivity to definite forms of disease,* we must admit at once that it will comprise groups of maladies which are very different in their nature. Of some of these states the causes are very definite and specific, whilst of others they are much the reverse. Of those which are most definite, such as leprosy and syphilis, it may perhaps almost be doubted whether there is any convenience in calling them diatheses at all. In certain stages when the disease is active there is assuredly no object in using any other word than the substantive name. It is chiefly when external symptoms are absent for a time in the individual, or when

we witness the phenomena of hereditary transmission that we feel to
need the addition of such a word as diathesis. It is in most conditions
easy to say of an individual "he has got syphilis," or "he has not got
syphilis," or "he is the subject of leprosy;" for the disease in each instance is a definite one, and there is no such thing as a state of physical
proclivity to either. Such maladies, however prolonged may be their
possible duration, stand in the very different category to scrofula,
rheumatism, or catarrh. These latter are diatheses which may vary
within the widest limits in the individual, and are so common as to be
well-nigh universal. We can scarcely assert of any one that he is free
from them, and the question is rather as to estimation of the degree.
They are diatheses in the truest sense of the word, and they belong to
the whole human family, and possibly, indeed, to all vertebrate animals. The more important questions to be put in reference to them
are not, have you got rheumatism, scrofula, catarrh, etc.? but rather,
in what degree are you catarrhal, rheumatic, or scrofulous? The degree
of susceptibility in each varies exceedingly in different persons, and in
many instances rises to such a height that it constitutes a very serious
disease. To these, so to speak, universal diatheses I shall have to recur
in my last lecture.

In the same sense that we seek to know respecting our patients
whether they possess more than usual proclivities to rheumatism and
the like, we also inquire respecting various other states. Has he been
injured by malaria? Has he been exposed to the causes which produce bronchocele? Has he a tendency to cancer? Is he gouty?
Has he any permanent peculiarity of the circulation giving tendency
to local disease, or of his blood-vessels causing risk of hæmorrhage?
In these and various other directions we see our way to the construction
of a host of diatheses of less importance than those we have mentioned
only because they are less common. In the present lecture I shall glance
at certain general groups of diatheses, arranged according to their
causes, and in the two subsequent ones I shall take various special
diseases, or isolated symptoms, and examine in respect to each how far it
is possible to make use of it as a clue to the diathetic state producing it.
Our knowledge of many of the diatheses is for the present far too vague
to admit of our attempting any satisfactory classification of them, and a

further difficulty occurs in the fact that their differences are often very dissimilar in kind. We might suggest a group of those which are transitory and those which are permanent, and others of those which may be acquired, and those which are solely obtained by transmission. It is clear, however, that any such grouping as this would often necessitate our placing the same malady in more than one class. On the whole, I think the simplest plan will be to make for the present a rough classification of the causes of diatheses, a task far easier than that of the diatheses themselves, and following this, I shall bring before you a few examples of each.

I will commence first with diatheses in relation to *climate.* Under the term *malaria* we may include all the various emanations from marshy grounds, swamps, and jungles. As to its exact nature we know nothing, but that, whilst similar in essential qualities, it varies in different localities, both in intensity and character, seems certain. Its effects upon the human constitution may be to produce quickly very severe disease, but, whether acute or otherwise, attacks of arterial spasm attended by visceral congestions are almost constant phenomena. Its effects, whether exposure be continued or otherwise, are always permanent. The man who has once had ague will display through life peculiar susceptibilities. Under all circumstances likely to cause shivering he will show especial tendency to rigor. He will shiver if a catheter be passed, or if he be exposed to cold, or if inflammation is initiated; and it becomes a matter of some practical importance to the operating surgeon to remember that rigors occurring to such patients are not so serious in their import as in others. They are retrospective symptoms, and reveal the fact that those to whom they occur have at some former period come under the influence of malaria. One attack of malarial fever by no means prevents another, and although subsequent attacks are usually less severe than the first, yet the effects of the poison are distinctly cumulative, and the limits within which acclimatization can secure immunity are probably much more narrow than has been supposed. It is easy to see that a poison which can be so persistent in its action and of which the effects, even in mild cases, are so well nigh permanent, must be capable of producing that state of body which we name diathesis. The malarial diathesis is, indeed, a well-marked one, and it exists in greater or less degree in all who have ever come under the influence of its cause. It is probably in some degree hereditary, the inheritance being, we may suppose, in ratio with the severity and length of duration of the disease in the parent. Inasmuch as the offspring of those who have suffered are usually born under conditions of continued exposure to its cause, it is difficult in them to discriminate between what is inherited and what is acquired. So great, however, is the combined influence of the two that a fearful state of physical degradation may be thus produced, and in this the inhabitants of a whole district may be involved. Nor is the physical health alone affected; the nervous system is especially involved, and the mental and moral faculties are largely influenced. When we remember how permanent in hereditary transmission such influences become, we can easily understand that the malarial diathesis has, in many instances, had a large share in controlling the destiny of a nation or damaging the character of a race. This diathesis can easily mix itself with any other, and in London practice we encounter it very frequently in association with that of syphilis, and occasionally both with it and that of alcoholism. I am speaking, of course, not of London residents, but of those who have lived abroad.

A climatic diathesis which must be placed side by side with that due to malaria is the one which results in bronchocele and cretinism. Here, again, we are ignorant of the precise cause, but we know that it appertains to certain local telluric conditions, and especially to mountains and valleys, just as we know of ague that it belongs to marshes. The cause of this diathesis is much more slow in its effects than is malaria. Far longer residence in the locality is required, and for its worst effects it appears to be essential that there shall have been transmission through several generations. It appears to persist with considerable tenacity in families which have once suffered from it. Like malaria, it degrades the entire man, and whenever prevalent produces certain deterioration of race. This diathesis may perhaps be most conveniently named, from its most conspicuous symptom, *the bronchocele diathesis*. It is absurd in the case of this endemic disease to speak of bronchocele only, since the general health is always at the same time involved. At the risk of being accused of repetition, I must here again insist upon the features of distinction between diathesis due to food and those to be assigned to climate. The latter are distinctly restricted and endemic; the others not so. The latter, when severe, affect all immigrants who come within their range of influence, without regard to health, position, or habits, and under certain circumstances leave scarcely any exempt. The diet-diatheses, on the contrary, as illustrated by leprosy and the like, affect immigrants only very seldom, and with great apparent capriciousness, taking one and leaving a thousand untouched.

These diet-diatheses constitute a group of great importance. They are persistent constitutional conditions—sometimes hereditary, at others not so—which have their origin in connection with food. Of them by far the most important for us, as English surgeons, is gout. Perhaps I ought to have assigned the foremost place to scrofula, and I should, indeed, have done so, but that it probably acknowledges a mixed causation. In many gouty patients the sum total of the diathesis is, as regards its causes, mixed. There may be susceptibility to weather, and to influences on the nervous system, as well as to articles of food, but these we can separate from what we mean by gout itself; and so far as this is concerned, I believe we must all acknowledge that it is a question of diet. About the intermediate steps of causation there may be room for much discussion and difference of opinion. But I suspect that no one will decline to accept the suggestion that had mankind continued to be vegetable-feeders, and never known the use of wine or beer, we should have had no experience of gout. If this be granted it is all I ask, for it is to be freely admitted—nay, expressly asserted—that such a thing as uncomplicated diet-gout is now scarcely to be met with. If, however, we can succeed in any degree in separating its complications from itself, we shall find in gout the best type from which to study the laws of a diet diathesis. In my own mind, leprosy stands next to gout in the certainty that it is due to food, but I cannot speak as to this theory of its origin as being yet commonly admitted.

Certain general statements may be expected to be found true concerning all diatheses which are due to food. They ought to be the same or nearly the same, in all countries where the same diet is used, and they ought to cease where the diet is wholly changed, and to undergo modification, or to become rare, when it is modified. To some extent they ought to be curable by abstention from the articles of food supposed to

be their cause; but we must not push this too far, since many constitutional conditions, when once established, may persist, or even become
hereditary, after the removal of their true cause. I scarcely need recapitulate the facts respecting gout which prove its association with
dietetic habits. They are too well known. It may be well, however,
that we should be reminded that the diathesis, when once established,
becomes by inheritance remarkably persistent, and that it is unquestionably the parent, when so transmitted, of many very peculiar maladies of which the affiliation might easily have been overlooked. I went
into some detail in one of a former series of Lectures in describing a
peculiar form of destructive inflammation of the eyeball—a chronic and
almost painless irido-cyclitis—which occurs only in those who inherit
gout, and I shall not now say more respecting this disease than that I
have, since my former lecture, seen some remarkable cases which sup-
ported the views then propounded, and none at all which were exceptional to them. There are several other less definite, and still less
common forms of eye disease which stand, I believe, in the same relation to gout, and with them I would ask to be permitted to place
(and I speak not without the justification of carefully-collected evidence)
a large number of cases of crippling rheumatism, almost all those which
are known as spondylitis deformans, a great majority of the cases of
gonorrhœal rheumatism, most of the severe forms of neuralgia occurring to young persons, and many peculiar liabilities to hæmorrhage. It
seems, indeed, under the ordinary customs of English society, very difficult, even after several generations of strict temperance, to get rid of
the gouty diathesis, and some facts would dispose us to the belief that,
even after it has ceased, perhaps, during several generations, to manifest itself in the typical form of joint disease, its effects may still be en-
countered in predisposing to disease of blood-vessels, of the kidney, and
of the nervous system.

The facts regarding leprosy are probably somewhat different, but
some allowance must perhaps be made for the circumstance that we
have not as yet had an opportunity of examining them so critically. It
would appear to be far easier to produce leprosy *de novo* than it is to
produce gout, and it appears also, as might be expected from this fact,
to die out of the system and out of the race much more quickly than

does gout. Probably it is associated with some much more definitely specialized dietetic poison than that which causes gout. For, if the hypothesis which I advocated before you two years ago, and in which I believe with increasing firmness, be correct, it is certain that the leprous poison is capable of considerable concentration under favorable circumstances, and may produce its effects in a comparatively short space of time. Many cases might be cited in which children or adults of healthy English families residing for a few years in a leprosy district, and eating only the ordinary food of the place, have become its subjects. Even in these, however, the malady is never rapidly developed. It always comes on slowly, and not unfrequently does not reach its height until possibly several years have elapsed after removal from the place where it was acquired and return to English food. This development of leprosy without possibility of hereditary transmission, and after short periods of residence in dangerous localities, is, I believe, never witnessed in temperate regions, and never excepting where it is well known that unwholesome varieties of fish are met with, and where also the wholesome kinds are liable to rapid decomposition. The fish theory assumes that, under such conditions, the special leprous poison may be taken in very efficient quantities in connection with a very small allowance of fish. It is the quality of the fish, and not its quantity, that we must regard. Next I stop to note that the same fact is observed, though not to the same extent, in the case of the beverages which produce gout. I am especially anxious to draw attention to this statement, because it is almost always forgotten or ignored by those writers who still disbelieve in the fish hypothesis.

As regards my suggestion that the leprous diathesis is not only more easily produced than that of gout, but dies out more quickly when the cause is removed, many interesting facts might be mentioned. Almost all authorities on the disease have laid stress upon its hereditary tendencies, but a great fallacy underlies all their observations in that these supposed tendencies have been witnessed in districts where the original cause—supposing that cause to have been a poison taken in connection with fish—was still in existence. Thus, it is easily possible that the inherited tendency may have been, at any rate, recruited from time to time by the original poison. The careful observations of Norwegian physicians in the United States have proved that leprosy does not persist in the families of immigrants from the leprous districts of their native land, and have further, I think, made it probable—although I do not know of any special cases that have been published in proof—that even the subjects themselves of leprosy get well after a long residence in their adopted country. I had the pleasure of producing before you, at the time of the lecture to which I have referred, an old lady who had, under my own observation during a period of about twenty years, recovered from leprosy. She had contracted the disease in Barbadoes, and had recovered in England. She is still alive and in good health, and has now had no sign of leprosy for many years. This was the first case of definite recovery from a severe and characteristic form with which, at the time of my lecture, I was acquainted. Since then, however, two other examples of recovery from leprosy—or, at any rate, a cessation of all leprous processes—have come under my observation. The subject of one of these, a distinguished missionary, now an old man, is blind and crippled in all his extremities in consequence of leprosy contracted in Jamaica thirty years ago. He has lived the greater part of this time in Canada, and for many years has been quite free from leprosy manifestations. I did not myself see him when the disease was extant, but the conditions which it has left justify the diagnosis, even if it had not been placed beyond all doubt by the fact that it was made by Dr. Brown-Séquard. Probably there are a great many persons living who are examples of the entire cessation of leprosy processes after long periods of residence in healthy districts; but no particular interest appears as yet to have been attracted to the search for them, and as the process of recovery is one which extends over such a long period of time, it is not always easy to recover data which place the original diagnosis beyond doubt.

Before leaving the subject of leprosy I must briefly summarize the evidence anew which leads me to place it very confidently amongst the diet-diatheses. It is the same in all countries, and probably has been so in all ages. It is the same in rich and poor, in hot climates, and in cold climates. It is certainly neither infectious nor contagious; yet it is capable of origination in those who go to reside where it is rife. It slowly gets well in those who leave its haunts and reside elsewhere.

It is not possible to mention any climatic condition which is common to all the very varied localities where leprosy is found. Whenever it occurs in a temperate climate it happens to those who are engaged in the fishing trade, and who live, to a very large extent upon the poorer kinds of fish. Although when it occurs in hot climates it usually observes the same rule, yet it now and then happens to those who eat but little fish. But this is always under circumstances where fish is known to be bad, and where it rapidly decomposes. Finally, in all temperate climates leprosy disappears before advancing civilization, the introduction of agriculture, and the increase of population.

Before we can decide as to whether *Scrofula* should rank as in the main a diathesis which is due to defective food, we have to ask what is meant by the term. In answering this question, I am glad to acknowledge help from the valuable lecture on this subject delivered before us last summer by my colleague Mr. Travers. The general tendency of modern investigation would seem to be to associate tuberculosis with scrofula, and to teach that both may be, and usually are, the consequences of inflammatory action in predisposed individuals. Much that is known as scrofulous probably never reaches a distinctly tuberculous condition. But the name is still, I submit, appropriately applied if the inflammatory action can be shown to be of that type which often or usually results in the development of tubercle. On the other hand, there are certain cases in which the proclivity to tuberculosis is so strong that it does not wait for the advent of an inflammatory exciting cause, but is produced, as a lymphatic neoplasm, without the occurrence of preceding congestion. In, however, the very large majority of tuberculous and scrofulous cases, a predisposing cause and an exciting cause are both present; the former being an inherited proclivity, the latter an injury, a catarrh, or any influence likely to produce local congestion.

The greater the degree of hereditary proclivity the less is the need for the exciting cause. We may note also that we frequently have to witness in the case of scrofula the influence of what may be called contributory causes, such, for instance, as the occurrence of an exanthem or other acute illness. We have then to examine as to what may be the influences under which a proclivity to inflammations of the scrofulous type may arise, and we shall probably be not much mistaken if we make answer as we should do in the case of rickets, that they are largely due to deficient and unsuitable food; but that, at the same time, it must be admitted that climate, clothing, and weather take each a very considerable share. As, regards diet, it is probably a deficiency of fatty matters, such as butter, oil, and the various other forms of animal and vegetable fat, which is influential; and, as regards climate, deficiency of sun and exposure to damp and cold. Scrofula, as we see it, is probably always inherited, but it is often probably largely increased by exposure to the causes hinted at. Possibly there are few practicable dietetic changes which would be more beneficial to our English population, in reference to scrofula, than a large increase in the consumption of butter and other animal fats. The comparative immunity of those who use the fish oils as articles of food, and the prophylactic virtues of cod-liver oil amongst ourselves, are, I believe, established facts, and their lesson is of considerable importance in reference to the dietetic causes of scrofula. We are enabled at the present time to speak much more definitely as to the diseases which should be classed as scrofulous, and as to their essential connection with the tendency to tuberculosis, than we were some years ago. A considerable number of diseases of the skin, of the bones, of the eye, have been conclusively removed from the scrofulous group, and placed under their proper designations, as cryptogamic in some cases, and syphilitic in others. So far has this gone that I can easily imagine that there may be some who think that I have given too wide a definition of scrofula, when I asserted that it is not always associated with the growth of tubercle. To such critics I will produce the instance of scrofulous ophthalmia, which usually consists of a chronic, slow-to-heal ulceration of the cornea, unquestionably dependent upon a constitutional cause, and often coincident with other scrofulous manifestations. There are also diseases I cannot but believe, amongst the inflammations of joints, which are slow, comparatively painless, in the ordinary sense of the word "scrofulous," and occurring in the relatives of those who are themselves tuberculous, but in which yet it is impossible to prove the presence of tubercle either in the bone or synovial membrane. The frequent and comparatively easy, and often permanent cure of many forms of scrofulous inflammation, is also, I think, another reason for believing that, although tubercle is its ordinary goal, it is by no means always reached. The scrofulous diathesis is indeed very ill-defined, and, in many instances, shades off very gradually into other states of defective organization. How closely, for instance, are many conditions which are called scrofulous associated with those peculiar states of feeble circulation and irritable tissues which give liability to chilblains, swollen lips, and the like affections? Yet these latter are not probably in any strong degree indicative of tendency to tuberculosis.

The liability to *Rickets*, in other words to a derangement of health, of which defective ossification is the chief, but by no means the only result, should unquestionably rank as a diathesis. It is one, however, which is usually, though not quite invariably, terminable at a certain period of life. In very rare instances, so rare as to be almost doubtful, it may begin during intra-uterine life, but usually its advent is delayed until near the end of lactation, and it reaches its climax, and begins to subside just at the time when the child, hitherto carefully restricted to a very few articles of food, and mainly to milk, is allowed to indulge its tastes, and to have variety. With such facts the first suspicion must certainly be that it is probably dependent on a milk regimen, and in the main no doubt this suspicion is correct. In numberless instances it has been proved that the milk upon which children have become "rickety" was distinctly poor in quality. The advantages in change of regimen are almost always well-marked, and although some experiments on the lower animals have failed in the artificial production of rickets through restricted food, others appear to have succeeded. Whilst, however, we may safely believe that defects in diet are the main cause of rickets, and that they may be effectual in the almost entire absence of others, yet it is probable that others are usually present and contributory. In the discussion on rickets which took place at the Pathological Society two years ago several speakers drew attention to the fact that the disease is very rare in sunny climates, although infantile inanition from poor food may be common. Mr. Spencer Watson in particular used arguments which made it very probable that free exposure to sunlight and warmth would do much to enable a child improperly fed to yet effect assimilation in such a way as to keep clear of rickets. We may certainly believe it probable that our climate and the narrow sunless streets of our large towns take their share in the production of what was once known on the

5

Continent as " the English disease." Let me here repudiate emphatically the suggestion which has recently come from Paris, that inherited syphilis is the real cause of rickets. The two diatheses are probably quite distinct, although they may often co-exist, and in other instances may simulate each other. Inherited syphilis,—as the labors of Taylor in New York, M. Parrot in Paris, and Drs. Barlow and Lees amongst ourselves, have shown us,—may frequently produce swellings about the epiphyses, and a state of general tenderness of the skull due to ostitis, which might be mistaken for rickets.

A word or two must here be said respecting a disease of the osseous system of great rarity which has been named " Rickets of the Adult." I allude to osteo-malakia, or Mollities ossium. It is probable that maladies having relation to different causes have been confused together under this title. But respecting a certain number of the best-marked cases, there appears good reason to believe that the disease is really a form of rickets, and that the differences observed between the two maladies are chiefly due to the very different condition of the osseous system as regards its development at the time of attack. Trousseau has recorded a case in which osteo-malakia attacked a woman of seventy who had been rickety in childhood, and another case in which this disease was cured rapidly by the use of cod-liver oil and liberal diet. There is a skeleton in the Brighton Museum which was obtained through the zeal of that accomplished physician the late Dr. Ormerod, which is one of the best examples of osteo-malakia that I have ever seen. The man had had innumerable fractures, and partly through faulty union and partly through bending of his bones, had lost more than two feet of his stature. In this instance the man's children were much deformed by infantile rickets. Although as an ordinary thing the diathesis of rickets, if not fatal, passes away as age advances, and under the influence of judicious dietetic treatment, we may reasonably suspect that there are a few cases in which it does not do so, and that it is quite possible for it to be reproduced or even initiated in adult life. In respect to its rapid subsidence, and usually its complete disappearance when the diet is improved, the rachitic diathesis has a close parallel in *Scurvy*. The latter malady is indeed of such short duration that we might hesitate to apply the term diathesis to it. It is for the most part an acute diathetic discase produced quickly and quickly cured. In saying this, however, we have not said all, for there are cases in which scurvy passes into the chronic form and becomes the source of permanent ill-health. When it does so it may fairly claim to rank with the diatheses, and it is quite possible that, in exceptional instances, some degree of influence from it may be hereditarily transmissible. In scrofula, rickets, and in scurvy, we have examples of diatheses produced by defective food, whilst in leprosy and gout we illustrate those due to some excess, or rather to something deleterious contained in the food. Close by the side of leprosy I ought to discuss ergotism, pellagra, chronic lead-poisoning, and some others, but time does permit. Can the specific animal poisons become the producers of permanent diatheses? This question must, I think, be answered in the main in the negative. Unquestionably they may produce conditions of ill-health which persist for a certain time, and may cause various morbid manifestations; but these states are short-lived, and perhaps are more fitly ranked as dyscrasiæ than diatheses. This is true even, I think, of syphilis, the most chronic and most persisting of all specific fevers. Excepting in some very small degree of reduced liability to the influence of the same poison which is to be observed in the offspring of those who have suffered, I doubt whether in any case the influence of a specific fever in a parent is to be traced in the offspring. No state of health which is heritable is ever produced. Some few exceptions to this should perhaps be allowed when smallpox, measles, and the like appear to intensify the diathesis of scrofula, but they are probably of but little importance. The general law certainly is, that a specific animal poison may breed in the blood, and may for the time produce most violent disturbance of the health of the individual, but its effects cease after awhile, and cease completely, and leave the body unmodified with the exception that it is no longer liable to the influence of the same poison. This immunity lasts only during the lifetime of the individual, and cannot be transmitted excepting in an exceedingly slight degree. Even in the individual it is by no means complete or invariable. I am aware that there is an apparent exception to all this in the case of syphilis. I will speak of that directly, and will also say a few words as to the limitation of the law of immunity of the individual. Before we pass to those topics, however, it may be well to ask attention to the

strongly-marked differences which are to be observed between the states
of health produced by the specific poisons, and those which are due to
inflammation from non-specific causes and which come under the law
of intensification by habit. In the development of such inflammations
as those of erysipelas, diphtheria, elephantiasis, and especially when not
due to contagion, the constitution of the individual takes a large share,
and the mere fact of their occurrence reveals his previous proclivity.
The disease originates, in part from without, but in part also from within. It is not an instance of intrusion, but of development, and peculiarities of blood, tissue, or nervous system, are exactly those which
are capable of increase. In the case of the exanthems, however, the
body of the sufferer is in the main passive, and is acted upon by a poison
which is intruded from without, and to which *nolens volens* his tissues
must submit. The occurrence of the exanthem reveals nothing and in-
tensifies nothing. It is from first to last a violence done from without,
by an external agent, and when its direct effects are over, the body may
be supposed to return in all other respects to its original state. A man
who has been put in the stocks is not especially likely to acquire the
habit of going to sit there, nor does the man who has been burned, or
who has broken his leg, acquire therefrom any tissue-proclivities. His
tissues were in no sense consenting parties, and the laws of habit do not
come into play. The possibility of second attacks, and the absence of
protection to offspring, are facts which indicate that the influence of
exanthems is only transitory. As regards the immunity of the individual, conferred by an attack of an exanthem, we may assume that
it is neither complete nor universal. Modified attacks may occur repeatedly in the same person, nor are second and fully-developed ones
unknown. Thus it is, I believe, a matter of general creed in the profession that, when scarlet fever is in a house, those who have gone
through it before are liable to suffer from sore-throat without the rash :
and that with measles catarrh may in the same way denote a minor
degree of protection. The modification of variola by vaccination, and
also the limited duration of immunity, are well known facts. Second
attacks even of variola itself may occur.

Remembering the length of time during which the effects of the
syphilitic fever may persist, we might perhaps expect that it would

prove more constantly protective than the others.   But the facts teach
us that we must not conjecture, but be content to observe.   No one has,
I believe, ever categorically denied the possibility of second attacks of
syphilis, but the opinion which almost universally prevailed, a few years
ago, came very near to this conclusion.   That, however, second infec-
tions with modified results are tolerably common, and second attacks
with full development of all the phenomena, not extremely rare, is, I
feel sure, the truth.   I have recently had under my care, at one time,
three patients in whom it was certain that they were passing through
second attacks.   In more than one instance the patient has been under
my own observation during both attacks.   One of those which I have
just referred to is a very remarkable case, on account of severity of both
attacks.   The patient, now a surgeon, of about forty-five years of age,
had syphilis when a student.   It was attended by a free rash, and was
followed by various sequelæ, which he did not get rid of for three years.
Then he married, and he now has healthy children.   In the beginning
of the present year he obtained by some accidental inoculation a
chancre on the lip.   It became very large, much indurated, and was
attended by large glandular swellings.   Subsequently a most copious
eruption followed, and aoth in primary and secondary phenomena, the
case was as severe a one as I have seen for a long time.   It may be that
idiosyncrasy has something to do with this exceptional recurrence of
liability during the individual's lifetime.   In one instance,—in which
I attended a member of our own profession twice for syphilis, first when
a student, and secondly, ten years later,—the same person had, he
assured me, twice had variola.   In respect to vaccination, it is, I believe,
well recognized that some persons lose its protective power much sooner
than others.   Those who, by an attack of an exanthem remain protected
through life, may be said in some sort to have acquired a diathesis.   It
is one, however, which, as I have already asserted, does not manifest
itself by any active phenomena, nor is it one the influence of which
extends to offspring; or if it does so, it is to an extent so small as to be
almost inappreciable.   It is a remarkable but undoubted fact, that
quoad the specific fevers the offspring of protected parents starts afresh.
It may be, and probably is, the fact that in successive generations the
tissues become to some extent habituated, and suffer less severely, but

still they do suffer, and nothing approaching to immunity is ever observed.

I have been speaking of the non-inheritance of the negative diathesis induced by an attack of any one of the specific fevers, but it remains yet to say a few words as to my assertion that none of them produce an active diathesis which is heritable. The only exception to this which will be alleged is syphilis. I shall be asked "Is not the diathesis of syphilis often transmitted from parent to offspring?" Probably it is not the diathesis which results from the disease, but the germs of the disease itself—the particulate elements of the virus—which are transmitted. It is transference, a form of contagion rather than hereditary transmission, which occurs. Two years ago I produced before you, at some length, the facts which point to this conclusion. Since then, by further thought on the subject and the accumulation of more evidence, my opinions on this subject have been much strengthened. We well know that the danger of transmission to children has reference not to the state of health of the parents, but to the lapse of time which has occurred since the primary disease. We see cases in plenty in which parents whose children have been quite healthy, subsequently afford conclusive proof that the diathesis still persists in themselves. Indeed, it is almost an acknowledged law that parents in the late tertiary stages do not transmit taint. On the contrary, when offspring are born in the secondary stage of the disease, especially in its early periods, it is a rule, with exceedingly few exceptions, that the disease is transferred. These facts strongly favor the belief, that the inheritance of syphilis so-called, is possible only while the fluids of the parent contain the living elements of the virus. These elements, in a large majority of cases, develop and go through the same stages as if inoculation had occurred at the time of birth. It is far more like contamination *in utero* than true inheritance. By contamination in this use of the word I mean that with sperm or germ (of either or of both parents), there passes the virus itself, the sperm or germ being itself unmodified, but simply the material medium of transference. In the case of the mother we know well that it is not necessary that the germ should have been infected at all, but that if her blood receive the virus, even so late as the eighth month, it will pass into that of the child also. Inherited syphilis, when produced under these last-mentioned circumstances, runs exactly the same course as when derived from a parental taint which existed before conception. A child then, I assert, inherits syphilis in precisely the same sense, and in precisely the same manner, as it may inherit smallpox. It inherits not the diathesis, but the disease. The reason why the inheritance of smallpox is very rare, whilst that of syphilis is unfortunately common, is simply that the period during which the virus is extant in the blood is very different in the two cases. The conspicuous facts, then, with which we are all so familiar in reference to the syphilis of infants, afford no proof that the diathesis of syphilis, any more than those of the other exanthemata, is capable of transmission. It remains, however, for us to inquire whether there are other facts, of a somewhat different kind, which support the view which I have endeavored to combat. I am alluding, of course, to the old controversy as to whether some forms of struma, and especially such diseases as lupus, may not be modified forms of inherited syphilis. My own belief is very strong indeed to the effect that they are not, but the facts are very detailed and very difficult to marshal concisely. My argument, if I have made it plain, has pointed to the conclusion that no minified transmission of syphilis is possible, that the child gets either nothing at all or the germs of the disease, and that in the latter case they will, subject to the laws of idiosyncrasy, develop equally in all cases.

Let me try briefly to state some facts on this question, and I will then leave it to your judgment. Nothing is more common than for parents who have themselves at some former time suffered from syphilis, to produce children who remain through life robust and in perfect health. Sometimes one or more of the family inherit syphilis, and suffer, it may be, severely, whilst others, usually younger ones, escape, and when this occurs the latter may enjoy almost exceptional vigor. When I have seen a whole family of grown up children, the offspring of syphilitic parents, manifesting signs of cachexia, there has usually been reason to think either that all had actually suffered from the full disease, or that the symptoms present in some were not specific, but due to other causes. I have seen very numerous cases of lupus on the one hand, and of inherited syphilis in young persons on the other, but I have never found the two things together, nor have I ever recognized in the subject of true lupus the brother or sister of one whom I knew to have suffered from inherited syphilis. Of the cases of lupus which I have seen, in a very great number there were strong reasons for denying the probability of syphilis in the parents. I have, of course, occasionally seen inherited syphilis and scrofula together in the same patient, but a large majority of those who suffer from the former never show any tendency whatever to the latter. In what I have said above I have been speaking of course of common lupus, and have wholly excluded that form of destructive ulceration which is sometimes mistaken for lupus, but which is from beginning to end syphilitic, and is curable by specific treatment. I have taken lupus as being a type form of disease, but what I have attested, as regards it, applies equally to other forms of scrofula, to psoriasis, and other diseases, which have been suspected as the remote consequences of specific taint. I believe that the domain of inherited syphilis is just as definite and just as restricted as that of the acquired disease, and that it stands sponsor to none but its own progeny.

LECTURE V.

Mr. President and Gentlemen,—In reference to malignant new growths it is possible to use the word *diathesis* as applicable to two different things. We may mean a state of tissue-health giving proclivity to cancer, or the state which results from the existence of cancer. I will ask permission to employ the word cancer in its old and popular sense, as including malignant new growths of all kinds. This is the sense in which it has been used for centuries, and it is, I think, a pity that it should be changed, especially as we have in carcinoma, as opposed to sarcoma, a very convenient term by which to distinguish for scientific purposes certain forms of malignant new growths from others. In examining as to diathesis, we must merge all the distinctions which have been established by the splendid labors of modern histologists, and speak of malignant new growths as one family. Indeed, it is by no means improbable that some forms of new growth not counted as malignant, ought in this matter to be placed with those which are so, and that we should estimate the individual tendency to new growth in general without paying too much regard to differences of kind. We not infrequently observe that some persons display more than one form, and when hereditary transmission occurs it is very common to see it produce a growth of a kind different from the original. On this doctrine of transmutation in transmission I had much to say in my last year's lectures.

The term diathesis is, I think, to be repudiated, as not suitable in reference to liability to the general diffusion, local recurrence, and failure of health which the existence of cancerous growth produces. These are all the direct and immediate effects of the disease, part of it, and are better named the cancerous dyscrasia. The real question before us is whether there exists any peculiar state of health wholly antecedent to the development of any local growth which gives proclivity to it. If such exists, and especially if it be in any way recognizable,

73

the term diathesis may be conveniently applied to it. The first observation to be made in reply to this question is that cancer in the main
is obviously dependent upon age, that it is in nine cases out of ten part
of senility—a sort of second childhood of the tissues. Amongst the
lower animals yet more than with ourselves, cancers are, I believe,
almost always the appanage of age. Old dogs and old cats get cancer of
the lip or mamma, but these maladies are scarcely ever seen in young
animals. When new growths which approach the malignant type are
met with in the young there is probably almost always a history of inheritance. If we admit this statement we admit, at the same time,
that there is a cancerous diathesis; since it is clear that a state of health
may be transmitted which gives proclivity to the disease, without actual
conveyance of the cell germs of the new growth. The probability that
such states of tissue-health exist, is increased when we take cognizance
of the numerous cases in which, with strong hereditary history, no
manifestation occurs until adult or even senile periods of life are
reached, though it must be admitted that these facts may be held to
be evidence in both directions. We shall probably be not far from the
truth if we admit senility of tissues, local or general, to be the one predisposing cause of cancer with which we are acquainted; whilst injuries
and all forms of local irritation are its exciting causes. A little step
further may next be taken, in the belief that everything which tends to
hasten senility, either local or general, will increase the predisposing influence, and in this category may be placed anxiety, distress, over-work,
and excesses of all kinds. It is highly probable that under such conditions a state involving increased proneness to cancer may be induced,
and further, that if offspring are produced after that state has been developed, they will inherit that tendency. This leads me to say a few
words as to the last-suggested cause of diathesis which I have placed
in my list. It may have seemed strange to some that it should have
been even hinted that senile changes can ever produce anything worthy
of that name. It was by no means my intention to propose to rechristen old age by the name diathesis. What had occurred to me was
rather this: Are there not conditions of tendency to premature old age
which amount almost to disease and which are sometimes observed to
run in families? The results are simply general tissue-degenerations,

—atrophies, arcus senilis, white hair, pale blood, and general failure of nutrition—and yet the causes are to be sought among the ordinary causes of disease. Both arcus senilis and white hair, when met with, as they sometimes are, early in life in many members of the same family, and wholly without other accompanying signs of senility, may be held to rank as idiosyncrasies of tissue, and imply little or nothing as regards the future. But there are many cases in which they are attended by other conditions, and in which they imply much. It is possible that arcus senilis may be in the course of hereditary transmission sometimes wholly detached from the state of health which produced it, and may become, as we have suggested that hæmophilia and xanthelasma sometimes are, heritable per se. More usually, however, it is probable that other conditions, such as tendency to arterial disease, accompany it, and that the total result is a state of premature senility. Certainly there are families in which a tendency runs to early senility rather than to any specific disease. I recently had occasion to amputate the lower extremity for senile gangrene of the foot of a gentleman who was barely fifty, but in whom general calcification of the arteries had proceeded to an extreme degree. I cannot but think that it would be convenient to recognize as a diathesis the state in which premature senility amounts to a disease.

. I wish next to ask attention to certain laws as to persistence, self-aggravation, and recurrence, under which morbid processes, due in the first instance to simple causes, or possibly quite accidental, may in the end breed diathesis. The best examples of this, which I shall be able to find, will perhaps be in such maladies as catarrh, erysipelas, and elephantiasis. Indeed, in what I said as to carbuncle, diphtheria, and erysipelas, I have already glanced at it. In our last lecture I contended that the specific fevers, in virtue of their own specificity,—and that they are intrusions from without rather than modifications of existing elements and processes,—possess no power of originating pathological habit, and thus do not become the parents of diatheses which are permanent. After a longer or shorter time their influence ends. In the instance of syphilis the length of reign is undoubtedly prolonged; still it does eventually terminate, and terminate completely. In my argument on this point I suggested that there was an essential difference in respect to this between inflammations which begin from particulate contagia and those set up by other influences, inasmuch as the latter do tend by the mere fact of existence to develop what we call pathological habit, and to increase in power by the mere fact of possession. It is, of course, not meant that they always do so, for fortunately there are other vital forces which are constantly working in other directions and tending to the restoration of health. What I wish to hint is that there is always a risk that an inflammation once experienced may become more or less habitual, and that its tendency is, if not counteracted, in that direction. In some minor degree this is true probably of all inflammations, even of those which have been caused by injuries. There are several ways possible in which local inflammations or local injuries may become the causes of permanent change in the general health. They may in the first place, by the long-continued pain and irritation caused, reduce the nerve tone, and thus stamp a lasting impression on the cerebro-spinal part of the organization; or secondly, by long persistence they may influence alike the blood and the nervous system. Sometimes it is not persistence so much as tendency to frequent recurrence which effects a similar mischief. Lastly, I shall have to maintain a theory that all inflammatory action is in itself infective, not to the same extent, but after the same pattern as malignant new growths. On this latter point permit me to go into a little detail before I proceed to the others. It is, I am sure, a fact familiar to all surgeons that, when acute periostitis attacks one bone, other bones are very prone to follow. Many years ago this curious fact attracted the attention of Mr. Simon, who wrote on it under the name of "necrosial fever." The affection of the other bones is distinctly secondary to that of the one injured, and not simultaneous. There is usually a considerable interval; and further, those bones which suffer latest never suffer so severely as the first. It is exactly as if from the bone first inflamed some elements had been shed into the blood having the power to infect others. The bones affected secondarily may be in no structural connection with the one first attacked—may, indeed, be at a great distance from it. Thus, I have seen it begin in the tibia and occur secondarily in the humerus, scapula, and ulna. The risk of implication of other bones exists only during the early stages of the disease, and is, I think, very seldom witnessed after the first fortnight. Mr. Simon's term, "necrosial fever," might perhaps suggest similarity with the form of multiple acute arthritis which we name *rheumatic fever*. In the latter, however, many joints are affected simultaneously and symmetrically, and all suffer in equal severity. In these features rheumatic fever differs much from what I have been just describing, and suggests that the different joints are affected independently of each other and from a cause common to them all. It is quite possible, however, that even in rheumatic fever the law to which I have adverted may be in force. We may remember that sometimes the arthritis does for a short time restrict itself to a few joints, or even to one, and that often some joints which escape at first suffer later on, whilst the implication of the heart never happens until a considerable time after the first outbreak in the joints. These facts would fit well with the theory that the parts first inflamed contaminate the blood and become the causes of inflammation of similar tissues elsewhere. It may be that it differs chiefly from necrosial fever in that the process is much more rapidly accomplished. At any rate as regards multiple periostitis we may be sure that in it the multiplicity is not to be explained by supposing that there is from the beginning some common cause, since in nine cases out of ten the inflammation of the bone first affected was caused by an injury. All who have paid attention to the development of eczema cases will, I am sure, bear out what I am now going to assert. It is very common for eczema to begin locally, from a known local cause, such as the use of an irritating lotion or poultice, the employment of washing powders, or exposure to heat, and for the eruption subsequently to become general. It is possible that the restriction to the part first affected may be very short, or, on the other hand, it may be very long. I feel that I may almost venture to extend the scope of my first assertions and to say that I believe that it is rare for a local eczema, if allowed to persist, not to become sooner or later a general disease. It would be easy to collect instances innumerable in which eczema beginning around an ulcer on one leg has been followed by eczema on the other quite independently of any ulceration. It is not extension by continuity of tissue, or even by contiguity, but reproduction of the same type of inflammatory action in the same tissue at a distant part. In almost all cases of general eczema there is the history of an early period in which it was restricted to one part.   I have several times seen diseases of the finger-nails (chronic onychitis) appear on several fingers and on both hands, apparently in consequence of an injury to one.   In these instances there is always, I think, a long interval between the injury and the affection of the other fingers, and during the interval the injured nail has always remained in a state of chronic inflammation.   A gentleman who had consulted me a few weeks ago for thickened and opaque nails, and in whom several on both hands were in various degrees affected, told me respecting one which in no respect differed from the others: "Oh, that has been so for thirty years; it was from a crush." I found that the crushed finger nail had been diseased for twenty years before the others began to suffer.   He had no skin disease, nor was there any history of such in his family, but I must add that he believed that his grandfather had had some affection of the finger nails.   It will be thought by many that this latter fact deprives the case of its supposed significance and reduces it to simply an example of hereditary tendency. I have no doubt that in most cases in which local inflammation shows a power of contaminating the system we must acknowledge the existence of a predisposing cause as well as the exciting one, and it is to this *rôle* chiefly that I should incline to assign inheritance in the case just narrated.   No doubt the cases in which local eczema becomes general happen in persons who have a proclivity to eczema, but this fact only reduces and by no means takes away, the importance of the exciting cause, since without it, in all probability, the morbid phenomena would never have come into existence.   The occurrence of eczema in any part and in connection with any local cause, must rank as a revealing symptom to this extent that it makes known the fact that its subject is one liable to eczema; but itself must next, if what I have suggested be correct, rank as a cause, and a very efficient cause, of aggravation of the previously existing proclivities.   Under this suggested law of self-aggravation the permitted persistence of any local disease may become a source of danger, just as we well know the permitted persistence of a malignant growth constantly does.   Nor surely is there any *à priori* reason why the life tendencies of inflammatory products and of those of new growths should be wholly dissimilar in this respect.   Amongst other instances of maladies which often begin singly and locally and subsequently become multiple or general, we have boils, sycosis, common lupus, various scrofulous affections, and certain forms of rheumatism. Respecting all these I believe that it is true that if they are cured after having persisted a long time, the patient remains far more liable than others to a fresh development. In some sort a diathesis has been produced. In the case of periostitis I have seen some remarkable examples of this.

We have now to consider the laws just adverted to, in relation to those which regulate the recurrence of inflammatory attacks. That certain forms of erysipelas are prone to become persistently recurrent is, as I have already observed, well known. We habitually recognize the fact that some patients are "liable to erysipelas," and expect that in them attacks will be produced by slight causes and that they will prove of much less severity than first ones usually do. If the recurrence has been very frequent the attacks are usually very short and mild; sometimes the intervals are so short that the disease becomes almost persistent. Exactly the same facts are observed as regards proclivity to catarrh in all its varieties. They are sometimes also seen in liability to repeated attacks of diphtheria, a fact which has been recognized by many writers. I had recently occasion to perform tracheotomy in an orphan school on a child who was *in extremis* from croup. In conclusive proof of the nature of the disease we removed at the time a large fibrinous cast of the trachea. The child had passed through, I was informed, four attacks of croup previously. It recovered after the operation, and has, I believe, since been threatened with a sixth attack, which, however, never became severe. There is a peculiar form of œdema of the eyelids and cheeks which is caused by repeated attacks of erysipelatous inflammation, and which results at last in permanent deformity. Of this I have seen many examples. In these cases the first attack is usually one of the ordinary form of erysipelas of the face, with the liability to indefinite extension constantly witnessed in the malady; but the later ones are limited, both in duration and extent, and the patient at length comes to know what to expect, and to be confident that the swelling will not go further than the face, nor last longer than a week or ten days. In some persons, and especially, I think, in the young, the upper lip and the alæ nasi are affected rather than the eyelids. The type of inflammatory action sometimes, as may be inferred from what I have said, ceases to be the most characteristic of erysipelas, and in others from the beginning it has in minor features departed from that type. Thus there is a form which we might call vesicating erythema which often affects the cheeks symmetrically, is of limited duration, and occurs over and over again. In some instances the vesication is extremely slight, or possibly absent, and erythema with œdema is all that we see. The cases differ from erysipelas in that there is little or no tendency to spread at the edge, and in some instances, in the comparative absence of œdema. They occur, I think, chiefly to the young, but adults and elderly persons are liable to recurrent inflammatory attacks of parallel clinical history in which the type of disease is rather that of an acute but transitory eczema. All those diseases appear to be for the most part catarrhal in origin, that is, the exciting cause is usually exposure to wind or cold. They are of great interest to us as proof that maladies which are probably due to very similar causes both predisposing and exciting may yet be attended by differing outward manifestations, and that, when once the type has been taken in the individual, the recurrences will be all of the same character. They also form interesting pathological links one with another, and between erysipelas and its allies. The morbid conditions which I have been referring to certainly establish in the individual who is their subject, through their long persistence or frequent recurrence, a state of health well deserving the name of diathesis, and there can be little doubt that the peculiarity so produced might, and would be likely to, become hereditary. We thus have occasion to note how a permanent and transmissible peculiarity of health may take its origin. Erysipelas has in elephantiasis a congener of great interest. The distinction between the solid œdema which results from recurrent attacks of erysipelas and the more characteristic form of elephantiasis is only a matter of degree, and it is well known as regards all elephantiasis that repeated attacks of rigors with erysipelatous swelling are constant features of the disease. One is tempted, indeed, to go the whole length, and declare that elephantiasis is, after all, only an example of persisting, or exceedingly chronic erysipelatous inflammation with its resulting hypertrophic changes. Elephantiasis may vary infinitely in degree, but not at all, so far as I know it, in kind. It always begins in œdema, and from this it slowly progresses to hypertrophy. The hypertrophy may implicate the corium and cellular tissue only ("smooth elephantiasis"), or it may involve also the papillæ, and produce the tubercular form. Usually these two forms occur together in different parts of the same limb. The solid œdema, which is its first stage, may begin from a variety of causes. It may be induced by an attack of *bonâ fide* erysipelas, by an injury, by any slight local inflammation, a chancre, an excoriation between the toes, etc., etc. Almost invariably its persistence is favored by the mechanical disabilities of the part, as regards the return of the venous blood and the contents of the lymphatics. We meet with elephantiasis chiefly in the legs, the labia, clitoris, penis, and scrotum, parts which, if once they become swollen, are dependent. The non-symmetry which prevails in a large majority of cases denotes the influence which purely local inflammation has in locating the disease. In some cases it affects equally both legs, and in these it may be taken for granted that the constitutional predisposing cause is strong. Such cases prove the fact of hereditary diathesis. They are scarcely ever met with in England, but only in those climates' where the disease is endemic, and in races or tribes which are peculiarly liable to it. When the elephantoid process has once well set in I believe it is never wholly cured; and no better instance could be produced of the pathological advantages of possession. The worse the disease is, the worse it is likely to become. It is emphatically a self-aggravating malady. The mere fact of its existence tends necessarily to its spread. Slowly but surely it undermines the health of its subject, impoverishing his blood, and mainly by the recurring attacks of erysipelas which attend it, enfeebling his tone. Constitutional treatment does but little, and local measures are the only chance of benefit.

We need not feel much difficulty in interpreting the phenomena which we witness both in recurring erysipelas and persistent elephantiasis. They are doubtless examples of the pathological power of habit and indulgence. Just as a man who has yielded to intemperance is in danger of becoming a drunkard, so it is with the tissues. The oftener they have yielded to any special process of inflammation, the more prone are they to yield again. No doubt but that, as in the case of the drunkard and the epileptic, so also here, pre-existing susceptibility takes its share in favoring both the first outbreak and the continuance. This share,

6

however, probably varies much in different cases, and may in some have been but very small. The main power at work has doubtless been the increase of proclivity which every recurring attack begets, until at length the habit or the disease, call it which we will, becomes fixed. Nor must we consider, as I have already remarked, that this power of habit will be restricted in its influence to the individual. If children be borne to a man after the habit has been acquired, they will almost necessarily inherit it. The certainty of inheritance will be in ratio with the fixity of the habit and the length of time that it has persisted before the birth of offspring. A great difference must be noted as to the inheritance of proclivities which are developed before and after the conception of offspring. If a disease comes into active existence only subsequently to the production of the whole of the offspring of its subject, clearly the latter will inherit only the degree of proclivity,—and it may chance to have been but very small,—which their parent may have originally possessed; but if born after the diseased process has been long in activity, they will take over the original disease much augmented under the force of pathological habit. Illustrations of this in the case of the children of drunkards are of common occurrence. It is all the difference that there is between one who simply bequeaths his patrimony as he received it, and one who has largely increased it by his own gains. Elephantiasis, although precisely the same disease, whether met with in temperate climates or in the tropics, is far more common and severe in dark races and in hot countries. Malaria has, perhaps, something to do in predisposing to it, and heat and moisture unquestionably aggravate it. It is possible, however, that we have much exaggerated our impressions both as to race and climate as strong influences, since the laws of inheritance will account for excessive prevalence to a large extent when once it has obtained its hold. It may be that we should regard it as to a considerable extent resulting from a diathesis which is heritable in certain families, tribes, and races.

There are certain phenomena which may, perhaps, deserve the name of *Revealing Symptoms*. Not but that all symptoms are in a sense revealing, but these in a special and emphatic manner, since they disclose the fact of the existence of a tendency, which, although present from birth, possibly has never been suspected. Symptoms of this kind occur, as might be expected, in connection with powerful exciting causes. Peculiar manifestations following the employment of special drugs, or the introduction of special animal poisons, may rank under this head. If a patient who receives the virus of smallpox develops a hæmorrhagic eruption, or if acne follows small doses of iodide of potassium, we may feel sure that in these occurrences we have a revelation as to the peculiar idiosyncrasies of the individual. It is certain that those to whom these events happen differ and have probably differed through the whole of life, from others in whom similar causes are not followed by similar effects. The touchstone by which these individuals' peculiarities may chance to be revealed are innumerable. The behavior of the vaccination sore and that of the primary sore often furnish to the observer an unexpected clue to the peculiarities of the individual. Sometimes the revelation concerns only the specific cause which has been in action, but in others it extends much more widely. For instance, I believe that a clean well indurated chancre without tendency to ulcerate or inflame rarely occurs, excepting to a person in sound health, and is far more common in those of dark complexion than in the fair. An opposite tendency on the part of the sore by no means always reveals or implies weak tissues or poor health, but it often does so in a definite manner. In making inferences of this kind, however, we must guard against the error of attaching importance to the state of the sore during the first week, which is usually due rather to peculiarities in the pus by which the contagion was effected, than to those of the recipient. The syphilitic virus itself is, on the other hand, always probably the same, and differences in its results are due to temperament, diathesis, or health-state of its recipient, and come into the class of revealing symptoms.

Some of these phenomena, deserve, I think, another distinctive name, and may be styled as *Retrospective Symptoms*. They reveal not that which is to come, nor even that which is present, but rather that which is past. In some cases it may be that their causes are still extant and influential, but in many I believe that the symptoms in question occur only at a considerable period after the termination of the activity of the influence which gave it birth, and that they imply little or nothing as to the present health of the patient or his future liabilities. They may, however, reveal a diathetic tendency, which by hereditary transmission may bud out anew in offspring. The explanation of this probably is that they are associated with diatheses which manifest their existence chiefly in middle or early periods of life. The term, *retrospective symptoms*, ought not, perhaps, to be applied to conditions which are simply the remains of bygone disease, however useful in a like way such conditions may be. It is rather to be kept for conditions which originate late, and which, like slow-growing seeds, spring up long after the seed-time. The best example which I can give of what I mean occurs in the instance of xanthclasma palpebrarum. When xanthelasma is developed in various parts of the body in an adult, I believe it is always associated with liver disease, and often with definite and severe jaundice. In these instances it reveals a still extant hepatic diathesis, plus probably some slight tendency to new growth and fatty degeneration. In the far commoner cases, however, in which xanthelasma patches are met with on the eyelids only, no such association is observed; a large majority of those who show them have never had jaundice and are in no sort of danger of it. Many, however, have in former years suffered much from bilious headaches, and if not actually from these, they have experienced repeated temporary health disturbances, attended by dark areolæ around the eyes. It is this fact which the patches in question reveal, and they may occur for the first time long after all liability to the disturbances in question have ceased. They are, therefore, retrospective, and I am inclined to think that in many cases they are solely so, and that little or nothing is to be inferred from them as to the patient's future. In other cases—and perhaps not a very small minority —the original liability still persists, and will continue to show its effects. But even in these, xanthelasma patches are usually the product of what is long past, and have required a very long time for their production. I have already spoken of certain other and very rare cases in which xanthelasma occurs in young children—possibly in several members of the same family—always in a multiplex form, and without any association with disturbed health. In these curious cases I would suggest that the retrospection is yet further back, and that they reveal the fact that some predecessor has suffered from liver disorder, or possibly been the subject of xanthelasma itself.

It is true of a number of morbid states which have received special names, and are often spoken of as if they were complete in themselves and distinct from all others, that their chief interest for the nosologist lies in the fact that they are symptomatic of diathesis. Their occurrence reveals the states of peculiar health into which the persons showing them have respectively fallen. Thus, as we remarked when dealing with the subject, enlargement of the thyroid gland, when endemic, reveals a diathesis which may end in great degradation of the physical state generally, and we ought by no means to be content to name it bronchocele, as if in that term we had denoted the whole malady. I propose now to take up in succession a number of names which denote according to custom distinct diseases, and to ask concerning each what is its symptomatic value, what does its occurrence reveal, how far may its existence help us to the discovery or recognition of the health peculiarities of the individual.

We will take first *Acne.* Under this name conditions which differ much from each other are grouped, but my impression is that the grouping is to a large extent natural, since they really are closely related. All forms of acne have this in common, and they are due to morbid processes occurring in or around sebaceous glands, and further, that their commonest site is the face, with the exception, perhaps, of white acne or milium, which is due to congenital occlusion of some of the gland orifices and accumulation of white sebum under a thin transparent pellicle of epidermis. All are, at one stage or another attended by congestion or inflammation. Their differences depend probably upon differences in the character of the skin in different persons, differences in age, and modification in the ordinary causes. In order that acne should occur, it is essential in the first place that the sebaceous system should be largely developed, and the skin moderately thick. These conditions given, we shall then be able to watch the play of various influences, local and general, upon their subject's health in producing its various forms. If his state of tone and vigor remain perfect, probably his glands will continue to elaborate and pour forth their secretion, without any disturbance. No accumulations will occur, and no secondary congestion around the glands will be observed. But the slightest, the most temporary disturbance of tone may derange the function of these glands, and may permit the retention of a thick secretion, or favor the occurrence of inflammation around an irritating plug. How rarely do we witness the occurrence of acne in any form before puberty, and how frequently do we obtain proof, after that period, that the influence of the sexual system is all-potent in so disturbing the tone that acne spots are produced. In girls menstruation is often attended regularly every month by fresh eruptions of acne, and in boys nocturnal emissions frequently have the same effect. If, however, the integument were originally thin and not greasy, then it is possible for the tone to be very seriously damaged by the causes adverted to, and yet no acne may be produced. In such cases pallor of skin may be the only result. In others in which there is less than usual proneness to inflammation, and perhaps very slight disturbance of tone, a peculiar form of lichen-acne, or very chronic persisting enlargement of the glands without congestion, may occur. This is seen chiefly in the temples and forehead, and in the male sex it is often coincident with similar long persisting enlargement of the glands on the penis and scrotum. The location of acne on the face is probably often explained by pre-existing peculiarities in the state of the skin of the face. Some get acne almost solely on the chin, or on the chin and cheeks, and these are almost always those in whom the nose is specially thin. On the other hand, those in whom the nose and skin generally are thick become liable, when acne is developed, to have the cellular tissue around the glands implicated as well as the glands themselves. Thus, tuberose indurations of a very chronic nature may be produced, which, if in adult life the causes of aggravation remain, may advance from what is known as acne tuberosa to the most grotesque deformities. Acne is very constantly hereditary, the same form often prevailing in several members of a family, and acne tuberosa, I believe, often descends in several generations from father to son. I have not seen acne tuberosa more than once in women, and in that instance a sister of the patient had common acne, and her male relatives had shown the tuberose form. The pustular or common form belongs to youth, the rosaceous or erythematous to adult life. If, then, we attempt to reply to the question "What does acne in its various forms imply?" we should, I think, have to answer that in the first place, it denotes original and heritable peculiarity in the structure of the skin; next, that its common form in young persons usually implies greater or less disturbance of tone in connection with the sexual system, and that its rosaceous form results from dyspepsia, attended by flushing of the face after meals. The tuberose variety implies original peculiarity of structure, and is often aggravated by dyspepsia and intemperance. Common acne is almost constantly attended by proofs of enfeebled circulation, such as cold feet, and often by constipation. Closely associated with acne is the liability to styes, to some forms of sycosis, and to boils. With these exceptions I know of no forms of skin disease which are due to the same class of causes or denote the same conditions of health.

A few words may next be said as to the symptomatic meaning of *Eczema*. This symptom is in a large majority of instances so far local that it is curable by local measures, and scarcely, if at all, by constitutional ones, whether drugs or restrictions as to food. Yet it is probable that there is always a minor degree of constitutional proclivity and this is sometimes proved to be hereditary. In a few cases, dietetic restrictions do appear to have important influence, as for instance, the forbidding of milk and sugar. I have already alluded to the remarkable way in which eczema appears to aggravate itself, and when once it has begun is its own source of extension. Probably a great many cases which become severe and general, might have been stopped in the beginning by appropriate local treatment. In most forms of eczema arsenic is useless, and this fact serves to detach it definitely from the psoriasis group. There are, however, certain forms of nummular eczema in which well-margined patches are scattered symmetrically over the limbs and trunk, in which the disease approaches very closely to a form of psoriasis, and is more or less under the control of the specific for that disease. Putting aside a very large number of mild or local cases, which are clearly due to local causes, we encounter severe eczema in the following forms: First, as a disease of the dentition period of infancy, or what is often equivalent, the lactation or milk-food period. Second, as a most persisting and troublesome eruption affecting only special regions in children and adults, as for instance, the hands, the lips, and the anus. Thirdly, as a general and severe eruption in advanced adult or senile periods of life. It is a noteworthy fact that when infants who have suffered very severely get well, they usually get quite well, and remain well through life. General attacks affecting the whole body occur for the most part near the extremes of life. Applications containing tar, if weak enough, will almost always both prevent and cure eczema. Sea air is often definitely advantageous, and the disuse of milk and sugar are often important. With such facts before us can we find answers to the questions:—Is eczema usually a sign of gout, or of any allied condition of defective digestion? Is it catarrhal? Is it due to structural idiosyncrasy of the integument? I should incline to reply that it is certainly not catarrhal in any correct use of the word. It is not produced by the common causes of catarrh, nor does it display the clinical course of all catarrhs, in the tendency to spontaneous recovery and frequent repetition. Next, in many cases it does imply a minor degree of mal-assimilation allied to gout, and is benefited by abstinence from beer and wine. Recent experience has led me to believe that the offending article is often milk, and to think it of importance to restrict it as much as possible. In very many, a large majority of cases, there is no true gout either in the patients or relatives.

LECTURE VI.

Mr. President and Gentlemen.—There is yet one other skin disease of such extreme interest in varied directions in reference to questions of diathesis, that I feel obliged to bring it in some detail before you. I refer to *Lupus;* and I comprise under that name not alone the common form, but certain other more or less rare varieties of the process, which I trust to be able to claim as certainly belonging to the lupus family. I am not about to trouble you with any detailed description of those several forms, but in order that the questions as to causes, relationships, and the diathesis behind them, should come clearly out, it is necessary that I should state briefly a few facts.

Concerning common lupus, then, I would assert that it is well known that it begins as a cell growth in the corium, that it always begins as a single patch, and always spreads at its edge by the infection of the adjacent skin, and that it very usually tends in the end to become multiple. Its multiplicity, as well as its local spread, is due to its infective power, and its secondary growths are almost always placed in close proximity with the parent one. It never in any case, however extensively multiple its patches may be, shows any tendency to symmetry; in all these features its clinical history resembles that of a local cancer. That which is true of the locally restricted form of epithelioma known as "rodent ulcer" is true also of common lupus. Both are slowly progressive new growths which after a time inflame and ulcerate, and then cicatrize. Both are curable by free measures of local extirpation and by those only. You cannot influence either except in the most minor degree by any remedies which appeal to the general health. Neither shows any power of producing gland disease, nor any tendency to spontaneous amelioration. The one is a disease chiefly, however, of early life, and the other of adult age. The varieties which common lupus presents do not offer us anything very exceptional to what I have said. According to the constitution of the individual, the state of health, the kind of diet, and the

89

climate, lupus may inflame and ulcerate much or little, and in connection with these almost accidental differences, the old,—and I trust now abandoned—terms *exedens* and *non-exedens* came into use. It may vary also very much as regards its restriction to a single original patch, or its tendency to multiplicity. Sometimes we see a single patch steadily spreading at its edge through the greater part of a long life, and never showing any tendency to produce new ones. This probably depends upon comparative vigor of constitution and a lesser degree of susceptibility. The explanation of the secondary patches when they occur is, in all probability, that they are the result of infection. As already stated, the multiplicity is never spontaneous. It is not, I think, beside the mark that I should ask attention to the methods of cure which have been proposed for lupus, as being indications of some affinity with the diathesis of malignant diseases. We have lately been taught by Professor Volkmann that every portion of the diseased tissue should be most carefully eradicated by the scoop. But his proposal had nothing whatever in it that was original in its theory; for long previously we had all been accustomed to act on the same principle and to seek by the knife, the caustic, or the cautery, to utterly eradicate every fragment of the new growth. If I am not mistaken, we owe to Mr. John Gay,—to whom surgery is indebted for many other practical suggestions—the radical proposal that the lupus patch should be cut out with the knife. It is essential that whatever method be adopted it be pursued unflinchingly and over and over again if needed. In this way lupus may be cured, and it is not too much to hope, now that this principle is becoming widely understood, and the profession is becoming bold in its practice, we shall before long witness a great diminution in the number of those who are disfigured by it. My object, however, in mentioning the success of vigorous local measures is not to enforce a lesson in therapeutics, but to intensify our conception of common lupus as a local new growth possessing infective properties. I might add that it often begins from some slight local injury, a sting, an abrasion, or a chilblain. Amongst the interesting varieties which common lupus presents we have a rare form, which we may suitably call "acne lupus," which occurs in scattered spots over the face, these spots being evidently connected with sebaceous follicles, and often with previously-existing acne pustules.

Their arrangement, however, I believe, never follows that of acne in being symmetrical, but always obeys the law of lupus, in that the secondary tubercles are more or less near to the parent one. In another variety, lupus attacks mucous membranes and produces slowly spreading ulceration, attended with papillary outgrowth. That lupus of mucous membranes as we see it affecting the conjunctiva, the gums, the palate, etc., is really lupus is proved by its very frequent association with well characterized disease in the skin. In another extremely rare variety, of which I have seen but a few examples, the lupus growth is exceedingly trivial, does not ulcerate at all, spreads rapidly at the edge, leaving behind it a thin, supple, and healthy scar. In yet another variety it receives modification probably from the part in which it occurs. It is but seldom that we see well-characterized lupus on the hands or feet. But we often encounter a form of disease which takes its place, in which there is less evidence of new growth and more of inflammation and tendency to papillary hypertrophy. To this group, the form of inflammation due to dissection wounds on the hands—necrogenic warts of Dr. Wilks, or necrogenic lupus, I think belongs. There is yet another variety in which the surface of the lupus patch does not ulcerate, and is not raised, but weeps, like an eczema, presenting a condition which would at first sight, and certainly by the inexperienced, be mistaken for eczema. The facts to which we appeal, in proof that all these very different looking inflammations of the skin are really lupus, are that they all take origin at a single spot, spread slowly but constantly at their edges, and whether they ulcerate superficially or not, always leave a cicatrix where they have passed. I do not think that there can be much hesitation in accepting the statement, that a disease which presents these features, and is not either a cancer or syphilitic, must be a lupus.

We have arrived, then, at the end of our first stage in the inquiry, and have seen that this peculiar form of new growth in the skin and mucous membranes to which young persons are liable may, while observing identity in essentials, manifest very peculiar differences in external appearance. It may be in single patches or multiple; it may look like itself, or like an acne, a lichen marginatum, or an eczema. These differences have more to do with the original differences in the texture of the skin which is attacked, than any other class of causes. Let us notice

the peculiar thinness and delicacy of the skin in the boy who furnishes
us the example of what I have called *lupus marginatus*, in which exceedingly little growth and no ulceration occurred. We have now to
take another step and to encounter another process with far more important differences. The diseases which are known as *lupus erythematosus*, and its variety *lupus sebaceus* are more than a mere modification
of common lupus. They are distinct varieties, or, if one dared to use
such a word, they are almost species. They manifest relationships with
other type-forms of skin disease, almost as close as those they bear to
common lupus. Had it not been for the fact that the common form and
the erythematous form, often exist together or slide into each other by
insensible gradations, we might have been tempted to prefer to call
erythematous lupus by some other name. Its most important difference
of feature is that it usually occurs symmetrically. Thus there is far
more reason to believe that it is due to a constitutional peculiarity, than
is the case with the absolutely non-symmetrical and local lupus. The
arrangement of the bat's body and wings, on the nose and cheeks, in
erythematous lupus is well known. The parts affected next to the nose
and cheeks are almost always the ears, and next to them the backs of
the hands. In this spreading there is no continuous connection between the patches. They are separate from each other, and apparently
independent. The evidence as to multiplication by infection is far less
strong than it is in the common form, though there can be not the slightest doubt that this kind of advance does take place at the edges of the
patches. Remembering what I had to advance in our last lecture in
reference to the possibility that all inflammatory processes may be capable of infecting the blood, I am unwilling to admit, even when we see
lupus erythematosus on the backs of both hands, whilst the whole of the
rest of the upper extremities and trunk remain free, that we have conclusive proof that these secondary manifestations are independent of the
original patches on the face. The symmetry cannot possibly be due to
any other cause than pre-existing proclivity of tissues; but it is just possible that it is not independent of an infective process also. At any rate,
it is true that this disease is wonderfully symmetrical; the ears, the
cheeks, and the backs of the hands show exactly the same conditions on
the two sides. The variety to which the name sebaceous is given is

often not erythematous at all. There may be no redness and no swelling, but the skin becomes dry, rough, and shrunken, and the orifices of the sebaceous follicles are very conspicuous, like the inner side of a nutmeg-grater. This form is also accurately symmetrical, but it rarely leaves the face. If you see it on the nose you may look for it on the ears, and in the middle of the concha of each,—just where in acne a group of comedones is often seen,—there will be a little patch of lupus. Lupus sebaceous and lupus erythematosus are frequently mixed in the same case, and they are probably the same disease modified by peculiarities in the skin. Although I have described them both as usually symmetrical, not unfrequent exceptions occur. Under all conditions they show their alliance with lupus by leaving the skin which they have affected in a state of scar. I suggested that lupus erythematosus had alliance with other skin diseases, and I was thinking especially of psoriasis and those modifications of nutrition known as chilblains, and my suggestion will now be that it owes its peculiarities to the mingling in varying proportions of these two diatheses with that of lupus. As regards chilblains, it is sometimes, when the ears and the backs of the hands are affected, quite impossible to differentiate between them and lupus erythematosus. The latter, like chilblains, is always worse in cold weather, and it usually occurs to persons of feeble circulation, in whom venous congestion easily occurs when the surface is chilled. Its alliance with psoriasis is shown, not alone by its symmetry, but by the fact that in exceptional instances the scaly patches may be seen on the tips of the elbows, with now and then a diffuse psoriasis condition of the whole surface. Children and young persons are but rarely the subjects of lupus erythematosus, nor does it usually attack those in whom the skin is thick.

I think we may assert respecting lupus as a whole that it is a sort of cross produced by tendencies at once to scrofula and cancer, and that it receives many modifications from peculiarities in the patient's skin and his morbid tendencies in one or the other direction. If he has a degree of tendency to the psoriasis diathesis it will assume the erythematous form, and it will be especially prone to attack the extremities if it encounter also the proclivities to chilblains. .

I have yet left for consideration another variety of lupus concerning which a few words must be said.   It is a disease which differs much from all forms which we have described, and yet I submit that it is really a lupus.   I know as yet of but four recorded examples of it.   The late Dr. Tilbury Fox showed at a meeting of the Pathological Society a young man on whose thigh were two different and very peculiar conditions— one being a congenital port-wine stain and the other a persisting vesicular eruption which had been developed at a later period.   As a result of microscopical examination, Dr. Fox believed that the vesicles in question were in connection with the lymphatic trunks and spaces.   At the same meeting I mentioned two cases in which I had for a considerable time taken much interest, but which we neither of us then thought to be ex- actly similar.   A third case has subsequently come under my observation, and I have now no hesitation in believing that the four are examples of the same malady, and that the lymphatic spaces and the lymphatic trunks are really implicated.   Whether it deserves the name of Lupus Lymphati- cus I must leave to your judgment.   All the four patients were boys; in all the disease had existed for several years; in all it was slowly spreading at the edge, and producing, near to the parent patch, secondary ones, which were apparently due to infection.   In none of the cases was there ulcera- tion, and in all the eruption consisted of little firm resisting vesicles which showed no tendency to rupture, and were aggregated into confluent groups.   Upon these vesicles and at their bases were little tufts of capil- laries which were almost nævoid in character.   By microscopic exami- nation of portions cut from all three cases, I have satisfied myself that the lymphatic trunks are dilated, and further, that there is a new cell-growth around them exactly like that of common lupus.   So similar is this cell- growth to that of lupus that a very able microscopist, who examined one of my slides, took it for a specimen of that disease.   It is right that I should add that in this microscopic examination I have been much as- sisted by Dr. Sangster, Mr. Robert Parker, and my eldest son.   My be- lief is that the malady in question bears the same relation to the lymphat- ics that lupus erythematosus does to the blood-vessels, and that it is an instance of a new growth assuming special clinical features in connection with the peculiarity of the special tissue in which it takes its origin. As in cancer everything depends on the tissue first affected, whether the growth is a melanosis, an epithelioma, or a scirrhus, so in lupus permanent modifications are stamped on the process according as it begins around the sebaceous glands, the blood-vessels, the lymphatics, or in the corium. When the type has been once taken it will be retained.

The various forms of *Iritis* are of peculiar value as indications of diathesis. Its occurrence in infancy, a very rare event, is usually indicative of syphilis. In adolescent periods, and early adult life, we have different forms of iritis, all of which generally imply the inheritance of gout. This inheritance is, in such cases, often modified by other individual peculiarities, such as feebleness of circulation and proneness to chilblains. When this is the case, a very peculiar form of multiple arthritis which begins in the last joints of all the digits, and often affects them exclusively, is sometimes seen. The explanation of last-joint-arthritis is doubtless to be found, as I have just suggested, in the peculiarity of circulation which in later life gives tendency to symmetrical gangrene of the extremities, as so well described by Raymond, and more recently amongst ourselves by Dr. Southey. It is not, however, due to this alone. There is always joined with it an inherited tendency to gout. The form of recurrent iritis which we meet with so frequently in adult men, but occasionally in women also, in which the attack is sharp and severe, the interval of immunity complete, and the recurrences take place once a year, or oftener, is, I believe, distinctly an indication of rheumatic gout. It does not very often happen to those who suffer severely from declared gout, and it is very rare in connection with rheumatism only. We meet with it in those in whom there is inherited proclivity to gout, who have lived rather freely, who are susceptible alike to weather and to diet, but who have never themselves had an outbreak of true gouty arthritis. The fact that this form of severely paroxysmal iritis occurs much more frequently in men than in women, supports the general statement which I have just made. In women of middle age, or a little past it, we encounter iritis in another form, as an insidious disease, attended by a little conjunctival redness, but with some sensation of heat and irritability, and gradually, without any definite paroxysms, producing extensive adhesions. The little exacerbations which attend it are often more definitely influenced by exposure to cold and wind than by diet. This form of iritis is, I believe, almost invariably a consequence of a remote inheritance of gout.

I tried in a former course of lectures to give a definition of the word *Catarrh* which should enable us to employ it for more accurate clinical purposes than it is often used. I suggested that it should be held to imply identity in cause, and not similarity in result. There is surely no good reason why all forms of inflammation of mucous membrane, attended by free discharge, irrespective of their causes, which are often very different, should be called "catarrhal." On the other hand, if we use the word in the sense which I contend for, we shall find it applicable to other inflammations besides those of mucous tissues. In so doing we shall construct a large and perfectly natural group of maladies. Whatever is the result of catching cold is catarrhal; conditions which follow from other and dissimilar causes, however similar their results, ought to be refused that name. The catarrhal diathesis, using the word in this sense, is one of the three fundamental ones. It is not due to any specific or any specialized cause. Every organization possessing a nervous system must be supposed to be capable of manifesting it, for its essence consists in proneness to inflammatory congestions excited, in a reflex manner, through the influence of cold applied to the surface. The susceptibilities of the nervous system, however, in this direction differ, as we all know well, very greatly in different individuals. These differences are hereditary, and may easily become the possessions of families or of race. Not only do individuals differ in the degree of reflex susceptibility, but they also vary much as to the special tissues or organs which are most prone to suffer under it. Thus, some catch cold, almost solely in the mucous membranes of the nasal passages and pharynx; in others, the tonsils, throat, and larynx are more prone to suffer; in others the bronchial mucous membrane; and in others the stomach and bowels, or even the liver. Although I shall admit rheumatism to the rank of a universal diathesis and place it for the present in this respect side by side with scrofula and catarrh, yet in doing so I shall have to suggest, as indeed I have repeatedly done, that rheumatism after all is only the catarrhal diathesis affecting the joints. Let me state a few general facts respecting catarrhal affections, and then pass on. First, it is a great mistake to imagine that only those of delicate constitution, and accustomed to much protection from weather, etc., are liable to catch colds. Farm laborers and others engaged in laborious out-door pursuits, often show this susceptibility very definitely, and suffer very severely. My impression is, however, that the peculiar degree of susceptibility which causes its possessor to experience slight catarrhal symptoms on every little variation of accustomed exposure, is rarely reached in them. They take cold but seldom, and when they do, it is in connection with some exceptional cause, and the catarrh develops with exceptional severity. I have, however, met with some remarkable instances of extreme development of the catarrhal diathesis in those who are constantly out in the open air. Especially well I recollect an apparently robust farmer, who could do anything he liked out of doors, but who could not sit in a carriage with an open window, or for ten minutes with his feet on a stone floor, without catching cold. It is a general law of all catarrhal affections, and well recognized in the experience of every one, that they are spontaneously curable, but very liable to recurrence.

All forms of catarrh pass off spontaneously after a while, and in many persons their duration is tolerably regular, and the period of immunity often keeps to the same average length. When we find the results of a catarrhal inflammation threatening to become lasting we feel sure that the diathesis is a complicated one. It is one which very easily mixes itself up with other forms of ill-health.

We define scrofula to be a state of the solid tissues, and more especially of the lymphatic system as a whole, in which there is peculiar proneness to chronic inflammations resulting in products more or less peculiar and specialized. Modern discoveries will perhaps lead us to believe that those specialized products are usually accompanied by the presence of particulate organisms which are neither part of, nor derived from, the original tissues. Be this as it may, we shall have to study the scrofulous diathesis, and the predisposing causes of scrofula, just as before. We shall still have to ask what are the conditions which favor, or otherwise, the development of the bacillus in question. Even the firmest believers in the new facts admit this. Looking, then, upon scrofula as a permanent and heritable condition of the tissues favoring chronicity in all inflammatory processes and directing them towards more or less specialized ends, it is easy to see that in such individuals catarrhal attacks may depart from their usual type, and may not show their natu-

7

ral tendency to spontaneous disappearance. As a matter of fact, we
are only too familiar with the danger of catarrhal attacks in scrofulous
subjects.

But it is not alone in the scrofulous that we encounter risks in connection with catarrh. Those in whom the tissues have undergone senile
degeneration and those, too, who although not old have become seriously enfeebled by other causes, often show an inability to shake off
catarrhal attacks, and a similar result is sometimes brought about under
the law of habit, when catarrhal attacks have been exceptionally frequent and severe. Apart from the risk of lapsing into chronic disease,
catarrhal inflammations are in themselves not unfrequently dangerous
to life. Many of the forms of acute bronchitis and pneumonia, and
some forms of enteritis, peritonitis, and pleurisy, are distinctly catarrhal
in their nature—that is, they result from the exposure of an individual
to the ordinary causes of a catarrh—and in many of these the popular
expression is verified, " he caught his death of cold." Rheumatic fever
very often, as is well known, acknowledges a similar cause; and respecting it and the other acute and dangerous catarrhal inflammations,
one general statement is true—that if the patient can only live through
the attack it will in due course pass off, and pass off completely, leaving
him again in good health. This remarkable facility of spontaneous recovery which is a feature of all catarrhal, or, in other words, of all
reflex nervous inflammations, has placed physicians in great difficulty in
coming to any satisfactory conclusions as to the relative merits of different plans of treatment. I will not say that cases of acute pneumonia,
or acute rheumatism, or severe catarrh recover as well under one plan
as another, I should be going far out of my province to make any such
insinuation, and I should be saying, too, that which, with my small
amount of information, I certainly do not believe. This, however, I
must repeat—that there is in each and all of the examples of this type
of inflammatory attack, a natural tendency to recovery at a certain
stage, which the student of therapeutics must always keep in mind.
Although I have spoken of cold, in combination with damp, as if it
were the sole cause of catarrh, it must by no means be supposed that
this is exactly so. With the changes in temperature there are doubtless, frequently coincident and very influential, certain electric disturb-

ances, of which it is very difficult to take exact appreciation. To these we must refer the great prevalence of catarrhal and catarrho-rheumatic affections at certain seasons, and during the prevalence of certain winds. This prevalence is sometimes such as to suggest, as in the case of influenza, that the air must carry with it particulate and contagious germs. The sum total of what are included in the meteorological conditions termed weather must count as causes of catarrh.

I have placed the rheumatic diathesis with the catarrhal and the scrofulous, as one which is universal, and in which all human beings share in some degree. What I have said as regards the laws of catarrhal inflammation apply very closely to those which are rheumatic, for the two are as regards their causes, very nearly allied. Rheumatism like catarrh is usually transitory, especially when it occurs in the young. As with catarrh, so with it, when the aged are its subjects there is danger that it may become chronic or even permanent. Like catarrh, it may mix itself with scrofula or be modified by any other influence which disturbs the general health. The effect of malaria upon the system is often seen to much increase the proclivity both to catarrh and rheumatism. One other diathesis so very frequently mixes itself up with rheumatism, and the two in hereditary transmission become so intimately united that it is a matter of considerable difficulty to ascertain how far rheumatism pure can go. We can, however, have little hesitation in admitting that it may be the parent not only of rheumatic fever, of transitory rheumatic pains in joints, fascia, and muscles, but of chronic crippling arthritis, in which almost all the joints are involved, and in senile periods of the slowly destructive arthritis which wears away the cartilage and eburnates the bones. Further, I think we may grant that it is not unfrequently the parent of sciatica and lumbago. All the affections which I have mentioned occur occasionally to those in whom there is no reason to suspect a gout complication; and, what is a still stronger fact, they are met with occasionally in the lower animals. Having said this I must not delay to add that in a great many of the exaggerated and peculiar forms of them which we witness in the human subject, the cause of the peculiarity is an hereditary complication of gout. When this complication exists it shows its power, we may suspect, by inducing a permanent modification of tissue; and it is to this modification that the peculiarities in the processes are due. Hence the impossibility, under many conditions, of discriminating between gout and rheumatism. We can for the most part easily tell, in any individual case, what the causes which have provoked the attack have been, and we can assign them on the one hand to those of rheumatism or on the other to those of gout; but we cannot estimate with any chance of certainty the previously acquired proclivities of the tissues. There is yet another source of fallacy, that we are by no means always acquainted with the condition of the patient's health at the time of the attack. If a patient already predisposed to gout, in his kidneys, his tissues, or his blood, be exposed to the exciting causes of rheumatism he will have one of those attacks which you yourself, Mr. President,[1] have so well described, and about the nature of which there has been some controversy. There will be difference of opinion as to whether such an attack should be called rheumatic fever or generalized gout; and the solution of the question is, I suspect, to be found in the fact that it is both. Two sets of causes have been at work, and the result has been a mixed one.

When a little white tophus is seen on the ear, the merest tyro can read its lesson, and the veriest sceptic dares not refuse its revelation. It is both retrospective and prospective in its significance; we know that the patient's kidneys have become unsound, and that he has failed, in the past, in the due depuration of his blood. We know that this loaded blood condition must have put him in danger of attacks of arthritis; and that in all probability he has suffered on many occasions from acute and very painful inflammations of some of his smaller joints. We know further that changes have taken place in many of his tissues, and especially that the walls of his blood-vessels have become thickened. Looking into his future we know he is in danger not only of other attacks of arthritis, but that, however carefully he may restrict his diet and manage his mode of life, it is probable that the renal and arterial changes will increase and bring with them their peculiar inconveniences and risks. We know further that if a man in such a state should have children, they will, in spite of the utmost care in avoiding the dietetic causes which originally produced it, inherit some of the

---

[1] See Spencer Wells on Gout, p. 66; also Garrod on Gout, p. 42.

peculiar tendencies which he had acquired. Where the inheritance will stop, how far it is possible for one structural peculiarity to be isolated, and to be inherited apart from others, we do not know. There is, however, I would suggest, good reason for believing that in families in which, either by accidentally changed conditions, or by intelligent foresight, several generations have been carefully exempted from the causes of gout, its existence, in times long past, may still be shown in the perpetuation of one or other, more or less isolated, tendency to structural disease. It is under such conditions that not a few of the forms of rheumatic gout occur, although in others, and perhaps a large majority, it is rather the fact that the exciting causes of gout have by no means been wholly suppressed. In this way we may have to recognize, as lineal descendants of gout, maladies which occur in those in whom we can by no means prove its persistence. I have referred repeatedly to the facts which favor the belief that the hæmorrhagic diathesis itself may, perhaps, belong to this category; and in a former course of lectures I analyzed the facts contained in Dr. Wickham Legge's able monograph on this subject. During the past year some very interesting cases have come under my observation, which serve to give support to it, and to lead to the conclusion that many, if not most, forms of intractable hæmorrhage are in connection with hereditary peculiarity of the arterial system, derived from gouty progenitors. I will mention only three, and these very briefly. A gentleman who consulted me a few weeks ago, with cataract and diabetes, told me that he had been most of his life liable to very profuse attacks of hæmorrhage. In early life they had been alarming, and sometimes so frequent as to be almost constant. They were always preceded by a sense of weight and discomfort at the epigastrium; and provided the hæmorrhage was not too profuse he had usually felt relieved by it. There was a strong inheritance of gout, and he had himself suffered from several attacks. A school-boy was sent to me by Mr. Harrison, of Braintree, on account of repeated and alarming attacks of epistaxis. They had been so profuse and so frequently recurrent that he had lost much of his color and strength. The point, however, which most caused anxiety was that his elder brother had died of it. In him the liability had commenced at thirteen and a half, had persisted for two years, and finally, after continuing for four days, it ended in death. Their paternal grandfather had suffered much from gout, and their father at the age of twenty-two had had severe epistaxis. In the case of a lady, now aged twenty-nine, and much out of health, I had the following history:—She had always suffered from indigestion and rheumatic pains. At the age of seven she had epistaxis to such an extent that the nostrils had to be plugged; and in spite of that measure it was, during three days, expected that the attack would end fatally. She once had bled to an alarming extent in consequence of tooth-drawing. Her first menstruation had soaked the bed through: and ever afterwards this function had been attended with losses so profuse as to have greatly enfeebled her. There had been much gout on both sides of her family, and she herself had had symptoms very like it.

I was unable, when examining this subject last year, to agree with Dr. Wickham Legge in his opinion that cases of remarkable tendency to hæmorrhage, occurring, as it were, sporadically, should be kept quite apart from the hæmorrhagic diathesis, in which we observe the tendency to prevail in direct descent through many generations.   It may be that as a matter of convenience it may be well temporarily to effect this separation, but it must, I think, be with the clear understanding that it is a conventional one. The hereditary cases are those in which the idiosyncrasy has become definite and established; the others show us the idiosyncrasy in connection with its original causes, and, if I may so express it, in process of breeding. The cases of hæmorrhage into the vitreous in young men suffering from constipation which have been collected by Mr. Eales, of Birmingham, and in many of which no history of gout could be obtained, go with other facts to make it probable that tendencies to bleed are sometimes met with in association with other causes. My own experience as to retinitis hæmorrhagica, blood patches in the conjunctiva, cerebral hæmorrhage, epistaxis, and other allied disorders, leads me, however, to attach very great importance to the history of inherited gout as their frequent cause.

There is one subject which it is impossible to leave out of the account in our estimation of the diathesis. It does not constitute a diathesis in itself, but it complicates them all. I refer to the changes in the state of the nervous system, or quality of the nerve force, which we know as *tone*. By that word I suppose that we mean the power of producing nervous energy. If we speak of the tone as low and poor, we mean that there is but little vigor in resisting irritation, and that comparatively slight influences will evoke a large amount of disturbance. That vigor depends, no doubt, upon the state of nutrition of the nerve-cells themselves, and it may vary much in different parts. Thus, the tone may be diminished in one nerve district and yet be good in others, whilst in some instances it is reduced in all, simultaneously. A condition of great general exhaustion is by no means, however, always equivalent with a state of low tone; it is necessary that the enfeeblement should pertain to the nervous system especially, in order that that term should become applicable. Perhaps it is further true that in most of the conditions in which derangement of tone is in question, the disturbance or enfeeblement has reference chiefly to that part of the nervous system which controls the circulation. Whenever the circulation is specially liable to reflex derangement, and congestions or their opposite, occur with unusual facility, we are safe in declaring that the tone is low. It is part of the business of the nervous system to duly regulate the supply of blood to various parts, to prevent local arterial spasm, and under the varying conditions of daily life to maintain the normal balance of circulation. When this power is deficient the various causes of disease act with greatly increased effect. In many cases loss of tone may be so long continued and so great that we cannot but suspect that it depends upon degenerative and permanent changes in the nerve cells. Not only may loss of tone aggravate a diathesis, but many of these act very efficiently in producing loss of tone. Thus the influence of malaria is very definite in this direction, and is felt through very long periods. But I cannot for the present dwell longer on this part of my subject.

The present is, perhaps, the most suitable place for me to interpolate two emendations on former lectures. In my first lecture I adverted to the want of observations for the purpose of estimating the relative frequency of the different complexions in the British population. In doing so, I omitted to mention the excellent work accomplished some years ago by Dr. Beddoes, of Bristol. I had intended to mention it, and should certainly have done so if I had remembered its extent and value. In a subsequent lecture I urged the importance of Life-Records, which should be kept in advance, ready to be produced to any medical man who may be consulted, and especially comprising mention both of family tendencies and of idiosyncrasies of the individual, and the diseases which have been passed through. In making this suggestion, which had long occupied my thoughts, I was not aware that the Collective Investigation Committee of the British Medical Association already has in hand a scheme for its realization. I have since with great pleasure been informed that such is the fact.

It is time that I should bring this lecture to a close, and with it will end my present course. In doing this, I desire, gentlemen, to thank you most sincerely for the very courteous attention with which you have listened to what I have advanced. Permit me at the same time to attempt a very brief *résumé* of the principal arguments.

We began by a glance at the praiseworthy and to some extent successful attempts made by our forefathers by looking into a man's face to determine therefrom his physical peculiarities and his liabilities to disease. On examining the facts supposed to indicate "temperament" I was obliged to conclude that part of them were merely the characteristics of different races; and another part, merely the products of past disease—personal or inherited. Thus it seemed that if race took its share, and disease that which legitimately belongs to it, there was very little left to be classed under the head of "temperament." As regards diseases in general, I suggested that the plan most likely to be productive of good results is to classify the chief groups of morbid influences, and to endeavor then to associate with each the separate maladies and tendencies which are dependent upon them. To this object our last three lectures have been devoted. We had previously endeavored to clear the ground somewhat by placing in a separate category a large number of symptoms and of morbid manifestations which take their origin in individual peculiarity, quite apart from any recognizable tendency to disease. I insisted that the domain of mere *Idiosyncrasy* is very large. I suggested that these peculiarities may have had their origin remotely in disease, but asserted at the same time that they have often existed for many generations in complete freedom from any such association. Whether I have succeeded in convincing you that it would be a convenience in medical teaching and practice to revive the old doctrines of diathesis I do not know. To my own mind it does appear, I may confess, that the states to which I have sought to apply that name are realities which it is very desirable to recognize. It seems to me, also, that the habit of naming diseases as if they constituted separate and complete entities has often a narrowing effect upon our pathological conceptions, and leads to the overlooking of special causes. My endeavor has been to look at disease not exclusively from before, but, so to speak, to get behind it and trace its origin. Classification should surely depend not upon external similarity, but relationship in cause. We should seek to place diseases in natural groups, in connection with their ancestral descent. The attempt to do this has, I fear, sometimes led me into speculations as to the genesis of the different forms of diathesis which may have seemed somewhat transcendental, and been possibly a little wearisome. I can only plead that I have done my best to avoid these faults, and I have been endeavoring to thread my way through the mazes of a most complicated topic. The main conclusions as to the diathesis which I have suggested for your acceptance are these:—That there are three great universal diatheses dependent upon the very commonest causes of disease by which man, and not man only, has been assailed from the most primeval times. These are—the catarrhal, the rheumatic and the scrofulous. Close to these come others of far less importance, but of parallel nature, because they comprise us all in their range of liability; the diathesis of senile degeneration and the diathesis of malignant new growths. Next we have certain very important ones which are widely spread, but by no means universal, since they depend upon local exposure or personal habits. In this class we have the ague-diathesis, the diathesis of rickets, those of bronchocele, scurvy, leprosy, pellagra, and gout. Respecting the diathesis due to *malaria*, I have some doubts whether it ought not to be admitted to the dignity of a primary or universal diathesis. If we go far enough back, probably the whole human race has been submitted to its influence, and not less probably has some impression from it been stamped upon us all. It may even be doubted whether now, in our advanced stage of civilization, those who are apparently exempt from all possibility of influence from marsh miasm may not still, in some minor degree, suffer from its remote effects. It is very possible that, although the severity be far below what is needed to produce an intermittent, yet that the well recognized ill-effects of certain winds quite disproportionate to their chilling power may be due to slight impregnation with malarial poison. As to the diathesis of gout, I have suggested that it is but rarely of pure breed. Very often it builds on the foundations laid by other maladies, and however much it may boast itself the *dominus morborum, morbus dominorum* it is, if we can see it aright, very often merely a complication of plebeian rheumatism. Other diatheses have been mentioned which it is difficult to place in any definite arrangement. That in which there is remarkable tendency to hæmorrhage I have associated, for the most part, either directly or remotely with the disease of the arterial system induced by gout. That which is characterized by failure of nerve tone I have linked in a like manner—not invariably, but still very commonly—with the influence of the sexual system upon the general health. So also of the state characterized by undue mobility of nerve force, or emotional susceptibility, known as hysteria. That there are hereditary diatheses which are characterized by peculiarities in the state of the different viscera, or of specialized systems, has also been suggested. In this category we have the hepatic diathesis, the diathesis denoted by chilblains, and that in which the vascular system generally is very feeble; and there results the liability to venous congestion in exposed and distant parts—even to gangrene of the extremities. I made no attempt at completeness in the enumeration of the diatheses, for it is clear that a little ingenuity might subdivide or define them to an almost endless extent. The description of a fresh diatheses is, in fact, almost as easy as the discovery of a new nerve centre, or the revelation of a new bacterium. Let me not be thought to speak in the least slightingly of modern investigations in the two latter directions. I simply couple them with the attempts made to classify morbid phenomena, and to say of them all that they are, for the present, tentative, and that the experience of the profession in the future must assign them their real value.

Finally, I think I may claim in all that I have said as to idiosyncrasy and diathesis, that I have done my best to recognize the power of hereditary transmission, and to insist that we ought to study disease as being, not of recent origin, or in dependence solely upon existing influences, but rather seek to truthfully "read the record of its long descent."

Again I must ask pardon, as I have already once done, for the fact that I have doubtless often appeared to be stating as somewhat novel, things which are well known and almost commonplace. I could not possibly, from the nature of my subject, have avoided this, nor, indeed, have I made much attempt to mark out what I wished to claim as original. It is abundantly sufficient for my ambition if, availing myself thankfully, so far as my knowledge extended, of the labors of those who have gone before me, I have succeeded in any degree in making opinion more definite, and giving emphasis to that which is true.

INDEX.

www.ingramcontent.com/pod-product-compliance
Lightning Source LLC
Chambersburg PA
CBHW022141020726
47496CB00008B/2497